Heart of Swine

by

Freddy F. Fonseca

First Printed in Great Britain by

Obex Publishing Ltd in 2021

Paperback ISBN: 978-1-913454-48-7
Hardback ISBN: 978-1-913454-49-4
eBook ISBN: 978-1-913454-50-0

A CIP catalogue record for this book is available from
the British Library

Obex Publishing Limited
Reg. No. 12169917

Acknowledgements

I want to thank many people who have accompanied me throughout this journey.

To those who are no longer here, I want to say thank you and see you at the next level. For now, you will keep living on in my pages. Thank you, Clementina, for your laughter, like a sip of fresh water, and thank you, Daniel, for your kindness. Thanks to my grandparents – Ti amo nonna, I shall miss you forever.

I thank my mom, the Maria who can create anything out of nothing. I thank my sisters: Carmela, who is infinitely more talented than me; Tiziana, always angry but immensely kind; Giordana, who carries the universe inside her; Annamaria, a painkiller for the soul; and Serena, a force of nature. And, of course, there is Giovanni, my brother from another mother, my everything.

Thanks to my friends. Without them, London would only be bricks and rain. Thank you, Olivia, Luigi, Muhammed, Nicola, Luke, Aimone, Rabie, Alex, Demi, Osvaldo, Vincenzo, Belen, Bobby-Lee, Sam, Henry, Yuan, Yifan, Eden and Rahoul. Thank you for the choking laughs, the love, the awkward moments, the 5 a.m. chats, and ultimately for making me feel alive. A special thanks to Ryan Choong, who has read and edited this novel more times than I have.

Thanks to Anne Karpf, Nandita Ghose, Trevor Norris, James Kneale and Ilan Kelman. Thank you for your inspiring lectures.

Thank you, Obex Publishing, for believing in my work and giving me the chance to show off to everyone for the rest of my life.

Thank you, Peppe, for your unwavering support, unconditional and often undeserved. You are the most incredible person. Thank you for existing. Love you forever.

Finally, I thank my father, to whom I want to say: HA!

Contents

Introduction

Heart of Swine is a postmodern dystopia set in an unspecified year in the second half of the twenty-first century. The story catapults the reader into a surreal world in which the ordinary becomes strange, unexplainable, and yet familiar.

Its dystopic elements are articulated in terms of surveillance, mind-reading technology, and repression, but especially in how the narration normalises ruthless individualism, excessive consumerism, and environmental catastrophes as the consequence of contemporary human behaviour.

Mindful of Marx's idea that history repeats itself, first as a tragedy and then as a farce, the story includes constructs of a future society in which behaviour, events, and emotions are nothing but a farce. The ontological landscape of *Heart of Swine* contemplates a world filled with religious rhetoric but inexistent spiritualism. It is a world that fetishizes material possessions, commodifies ideals, and commercialises poverty. The deliberately absurd and sarcastic descriptions of events, foods, character reactions and dialogue will entertain the reader while showcasing the possible cacotopia the future holds.

December 30, 2027.

I know the truth.

THE TRUEST OF THE TRUTHS

- *2017:* *Russia cuts off the gas as snowstorms hit Europe. Citizens freeze to* **death***. Our dearest President Manson comes up with a solution: investing in the meat industry. Of course, this would mean trusting vegans and their blog posts about how the emissions from the meat plants lead to a temperature rise, but it's worth a shot. The slaughter of the animals seems to follow* **the Chinese zodiac***. 2017 is the year of the Rooster. The* **Chickenocide** *lasts for two years.*

- *2019:* *Year of the Pig. The government promotes* **The Bacon Wave** *through a series of well-calculated Twitter storms and a mediatic avalanche of Tastyy videos showing the happiest ending for a pig: bacon chains, bacon party decorations, #BeconMyValentine for the romantics. As predicted, the sulphur and carbon dioxide emissions from the meat plants successfully lead to a* **global temperature rise.**

- *2023:* *No more winters. Meteorologists register storms of* **hot rain** *around the planet. The levels of oxygen plummet— many die; those who survive must learn how to get used to breathing carbon dioxide. On the downside, the rising* *sea level threatens to wipe off the coasts of England. Our dearest President Manson decides to solve the problem by draining the sea and filtering ocean water for irrigations. He buys avocado plantations in South America, financing a farmer Stakhanovite movement. The more they produce, the more first-world goods they receive: Nike hair bands, Marc Jacobs credit card holders, Chanel nail polish and even a luminous hoverboard for whoever is able to collect 1000 avocados in 24 hours. Some die of fatigue, others from severe injuries after trying to protect their baskets from over-excited Stakhanovites.*

Avocados are now in great demand, possibly because of an extensive marketing campaign and undoubtedly because of the chemical stimulants added to the fruits, making them as addictive as crack cocaine.

- *2025: The flourishing avocado business becomes unsustainable; the demand is so high that farmers now use drinking water for their plantations. Despite their efforts, the production cannot keep up with the demand. A progressive shortage of avocados and the delays in the deliveries to the U.K. generate the so-called 'avocado tourism'. Sellers, businessmen and even entire families start their peregrinations to South America to ensure they get their share of avocados.*

- *2026: The reserves **of avocados progressively diminish, leading to the Great Avocado War,** a series of violent clashes between over-excited avocado tourists and plantation workers. Tired of their inhumane living conditions and the Stakhanovism imposed upon them, farmers organised a series of guerrilla operations against the tourists. Millions die. The U.K. decrees 50 years of silence in respect for the **victims of the conflict.** Journalists and conspiracy theorists*

3

who try to investigate the matter are imprisoned and charged with Mansonism (**subversion and treason**).

If you are reading, my dears,
I do not know how long
I have left.

THE BEGINNING OF THE BEGINNING

'Ever since he was born, I could see he was special. A real gentleman, you know.'

'When was that?'

'April 20, 2022. One day old and already taking care of his siblings. He always allowed them to feed first. And he only sucked from the third nipple. Please don't ask me why; I have no idea. Maybe it's because…'

'Mr Marxim, please let's stick to the facts. So, in 2022… he's now a grown-up. Any hormonal crisis or rebellious tattoo our readers would need to know about?'

'Oh no, only one, but that wasn't really his choice, I guess.'

'Meaning?'

'A herd mark.'

'Right. Anything unusual while he was growing up?'

Mr Marxim hesitated, thinking about something exciting or more like something sensational to say.

'I couldn't keep him out of the house when he was younger. He was always snooping around my encyclopaedias. Of course, he couldn't read because …'

'Because he's a pig,' the reporter continued.

'No,' insisted Marxim through clenched teeth before his tone softened like a mother talking about her favourite child. 'Because he was just so young. But he loved looking at the pictures, and with his hoof, he used to scratch the pages he liked more, all while his siblings were just rolling in the mud all day, grunting when they were hungry or when they felt like it.'

'Oh, siblings … how wonderful. Nobody has ever written about his siblings. Would it be possible to talk to them?'

'Impossible.'

'I am sorry, of course. I meant, would it be possible to see them? You know, I think seeing them would give a much more interesting nuance to the story. It would humanise–'

Marxim slammed his fists on his old armchair as he shouted. 'I said no!'

'Why is that?' The reporter, Chekhovich, stopped scribbling on his notebook and finally looked Mr Marxim in the face.

Marxim could see his sinful face – his sinful, murderous face in the reflection of the reporter's glasses.

'Well, I am not proud to say it, but you know, it was a different time. I didn't know any better.'

'Mr Marxim, what did you do with his siblings? Where is his mom?' Chekhovich's eyes lit with journalistic ambition.

Marxim couldn't stand looking at his reflection. He turned his face to the window where the grass lulled by the wind seemed to calm his anguish. A feeble oink echoed in his head. He saw a sounder of pigs running towards the house as a younger Marxim whistled, *lunch is ready*. The pigs, Pinkish and Happy, shook their little tails and tried to take playful bites at Marxim's arm, which he stretched and retracted and used to surprise the pigs with sonorous smacks on their backs. The good old days. Another smack reverberated in his head, and a more sinister memory played in front of his eyes. As his guilt turned the sky grey, he saw himself slapping the pigs to speed them up onto the truck that would take them to hell first and then to supermarkets and restaurants afterwards.

Chekhovich clapped his hands. 'Are you still with me?'

'Back then, everybody was doing it, OK? It's not my fault.'

'What have you done with his family?'

'OK, maybe it is my fault, but I regret it. I know I have sinned. Don't I deserve forgiveness? Isn't it like a sacrament to forgive and forget?'

'I am not a religious man, but I am pretty sure it's not a sacrament.'

'What do you mean it's not a sacrament? Forgive- forget-forbid-for ... what was the other? Well, he forgave me, anyway, so why shouldn't you?'

'Marxim. Sorry, can I call you Marxim?' the reporter said, taking off his glasses. 'Look, I am not judging you. Just tell me what happened.'

Marxim nodded, sipping the now cold Earl Grey tea with lemon, not milk, which had stayed untouched on the table since the beginning of the interview. The tea was as bitter as his old, worn, and most unusual green eyes, yellowish skin, and ginger hair. However, like his appearance, he was long used to it by now. Perhaps too used to it, if that were possible.

He wore a denim dungaree with a white undershirt and orange plastic boots. He looked just like a real farmer, an actual old and genuine farmer.

'So, Marxim, you were saying …'

'Nothing, I … You know, it was 2019, and everybody was doing it … eating meat. I mean, humans have eaten meat since the beginning of time. What do you think all the fuss was about between Cain and Abel? They fought for a lamb chop. Anyway, that was the year the Bacon Wave hit the world. I don't know how it started, but everybody was obsessed with bacon. I was too. You might be too young to remember, but we had everything with bacon. Channels were showing all kinds of recipes with bacon. Bacon, bacon, bacon … crispy, tasty … No. I gotta stay strong,' said Marxim slapping himself on the face.

'I remember, those were dark years. It was almost in the same period of the Great Avocado War if I'm not mistaken.'

'Oh yeah, I remember that. It was a guac'a murder bath. Luckily, I don't have any avocado trees on my farm; that would have ruined me.'

'So, going back to the siblings …'

'Yeah, well, you know, I waited for as long as I could, but then pigs started to get rarer and rarer. They were called pink gold in the industry.'

'You sold them, I imagine.'

'Well, yes, but I made sure they didn't suffer.'

'What do you mean?'

'I drugged them before they … you know.'

'And why didn't you sell the captain with them?'

'I don't know. I have always had a special connection with Captain Grunter.'

'Did you keep him as your personal bacon stash?'

'How dare you!' Marxim's anger and shame burned vehemently on his cheeks. 'He's like a son to me. I never got married or had any kids. But with Oink-Oinkster, it was like what I think having a son must feel like,' Marxim's guilty mouth added.

'Sweet. Where is he now?'

'I think he's in the bedroom. I could call him if you want …'

'No. No need for that. I think I got everything I need.' He stepped closer to Marxim, and they shook hands.

'What did you say your name is?'

'Chekhovich, Chekhov Chekhovich,' the reporter said, putting his sunglasses back on.

Marxim escorted the reporter out, repeating his name and failing miserably. As he opened the door, the torrid air entered the house. Chekovich was out before he could even say goodbye. The sun was high in the sky. Marxim checked the clock, 12:00 on the dot; it was time for lunch now.

***

'The sun is high in the sky; it must be noon. I can't wait to go home. I got all the material for the ... Fuck!'

A not very promising squishy sound played under Chekhovich's foot. The reporter took his sunglasses off to see what he had stepped on. His vintage plastic black shoes were ruined. Then, with a leaf wrapped around his finger, he analysed the composition of the soggy, greenish puddle.

Strange ... It really looks like chicken shit.

Slightly confused, he kept walking, despite the tree branches that kept slapping him and the hot pebbles slowly making their way into his shoes. He didn't have time to stop and swear; he just wanted to get home before he forgot the headline for the piece about Captain Grunter.

It was only when he arrived at his old car, a BMW X5, that he remembered something he read at Barbuccio-Hair&Beard (*for females too*) three Wednesdays before. He had an appointment to trim his eyelashes, but Barbuccio had gone for his lunch break when he got to the shop. Italians, right? While he waited for Barbuccio to come back, he started scavenging in a box full of old newspapers, trying to find something readable. The news was not printed on paper anymore, and it was hard to readjust to the old ways. Many of the papers he found were first editions of '*A'lex*,' which he avoided. Then he found a '*Gazelle Gazette*.' He remembered getting comfortable in the chair and cursing Barbuccio as he started reading.

'Scientists have modelled factors driving the mainland chicken population decline and are calling for action to reduce regional and international threats. According to the researchers' prediction models, breeding success of the bird will continue to decline; the species is likely to be extinct by 2021 due to the rising chicken roll consumption.'

Every chicken must be dead by now. It was probably something else's shit.

Chekhovich couldn't get that thought out of his head as he started the car. The seatbelt alarm started beeping.

'Who even has a seatbelt in their car nowadays?' he said between his teeth as the vein on his forehead got bigger.

As he continued towards his apartment, the blue sky turned grey, then darker grey, and it started to rain. Boiling water came down from the angry sky and threatened to blister the already ravaged car paint. On the street, the dirt became a stream that poured down the manhole.

The rain cleaned everything, at least on the surface.

'With every rain, a new start. For every pain, Mozart.' Read a poster on Montague Street.

He turned on the radio. From Monday to Friday, all the stations played Mozart, but it was a free choice during the weekend – meaning the greatest hits of Ariana Grande and Bad Bunny. This rigorous programme was part of an initiative meant to boost productivity in the workplace and promote the 'work hard, play harder' philosophy.

The stereo played 'Requiem' in D minor. Chekhovich started thinking about Marxim's words. Like how the Bacon Wave exterminated all those poor pigs, those poor, delicious, full-flavoured pigs, and how after thousands of years of "moderate" pork consumption, people became so addicted to bacon in 2019. How was that possible? Did that mean anything?

Those were dark years for the swine, but somehow, Marxim saved the only super-pig that ever existed. And what a little miracle! People said that Captain Grunter was going to bring peace to Earth. They wished the captain had been around for the Great Avocado War. How many lives could he have saved? How many avocados would he have spared? Who knows, maybe he might have done something about the Chickenocide too.

Chekhovich's head started spinning. Sometimes, he felt like he was thinking too hard. At some point, things usually kind of made sense in a perplexed and often forgetful way. It was like his thoughts were flashing through his head at warp speed, and he couldn't get hold of them. He felt a kind of warmth inside. He experienced the same feeling whenever he knew the answer to the million-dollar question the professor had posed in class. He began to gasp for air, his face got purple, and his heart's rapid beating echoed so loudly in his head until he forgot what he wanted to say. Chekhovich turned off the engine and focused on taking deep breaths. He was going to follow through – he wasn't sure with what, but he was going to. Something didn't add up: Bacon Wave, Chickenocide, and Avocado War. Everything was just too odd, but to be fair, Mozart's Requiem in D minor could turn everything into a conspiracy.

When he finally arrived home, Chekhovich opened the kitchen's cupboards as if he didn't know they were empty. He got some coffee and switched on his laptop. With his thoughts, he started navigating the Ether, looking for some 'Tastyy' clips. All he needed to placate his hunger was to look at these haute cuisine videos. He even had a favourite: 'Orange Parmesan Truffles Filled with Strawberry Barbecue Sauce.'

He watched the video a couple of times until he shivered, regurgitating the coffee.

His mind went back to the Bacon Wave, and before he could stop it, his laptop had found more than 13,790,000,000 results. He started reading; he would have to write his article later.

***

Five days later, all over the city, giant boards shone with the headline of the article in red and yellow:

CAPTAIN GRUNTER AND SAVIOUR MARXIM: A KINKY LOVE STORY

(*Make sure you subscribe to A'lex's news today. YES! We accept mind payments!*)

Like every morning, Captain Grunter was drifting around the city to check that the levels of CO_2 weren't too low. As all beings evolved, the human body got so used to carbon dioxide that the lungs couldn't properly work now with oxygen. Too much of it caused respiratory failure; thousands died every year. As he floated through the air, his peachy ears sparkled under the sunlight, and drool fell from his mouth, which was hanging ajar, blessing the lucky passers-by on the head.

Close to New-Old Street, Captain Grunter saw the billboard advertising the article about him. The blood in his veins froze till it started boiling. He grunted in howls and sped up while flies and pigeons crashed into him. The sky became a wire fence database of A'lex's employees. While processing the information, he summoned Marxim, who materialised at high speed atop the captain, and almost fell from his back. He found his target at Chekhov Chekhovich, 9 Dream House, Shadwell.

***

'Please! I had to write the article. Wait – I swear, A'lex made me.' The begging Chekhovich, crying and moaning humbly, lifted his hands. 'Please, no!'

The captain started loading his hoofs, his eyes turning green. Marxim's yellow face went yellower. He was still sick from the ride, but apart from that, he didn't really care about what was happening.

'I have some information that might interest you.'

Chekhovich dried his runny nose.

'Wait,' Marxim pulled the captain's ear, 'let the piece of crap talk.'

The pig unloaded the hoofs.

'I am sorry about the article. They made me write it.'

'They made you? Who made you?' Marxim asked.

'Well ... ehm, the economy. I gotta pay rent. My–'

Marxim blew a raspberry. 'I think it's time to flush.'

'I have information about the Bacon Wave ...'

The captain lowered his head, grunting something.

'Think about it: how is it possible that 99% of the pig population was consumed in a few years? I mean, why? How?'

'Tell us what you have found,' Marxim said impatiently.

'OK, sit here. I will show you,' said Chekhovich, soon regretting his offer and frowning while looking at the dirty hoofs on his no longer pristine white sheets.

'Let me just connect my mind to the projector.'

The captain and Marxim nodded.

'OK, let's begin from … Well, let's begin from the beginning. In 2018, the first 'Tastyy' video came out. Its recipes: roasted chicken filled with bacon and wrapped in bacon. Delicious, no offence. Then, the power pork patty burger wrapped with bacon, the one-million-calories bacon lasagne, bacon cupcakes…'

Images of sliced, grounded, sizzled pigs played across the room, mentally projected onto the walls.

While Chekhovich salivated watching his dream dinners prepared in front of his eyes, Captain Grunter saw the tragedy of two soulmates united in a pan of hot grease and barbecue sauce. The sizzling that made Marxim's spine shiver with excitement was an agonizing scream for Captain Grunter.

He watched the carcasses of brothers and sisters ravaged with surgical precision, legs and organs passed through a grinder; there was no blood dripping from the flesh. They strategically removed anything that could have disturbed a sensible audience. If there was no blood, there was no suffering. Instead, a new real had been created. Pigs turned into pork, and they were no longer living beings but just objects: cubes, loins, tenderloins, and necklaces of sausages that, while being cooked, kept shrinking as a final act of humiliation.

Pigs cooked whole, a stick stuck in their asshole, and off they went, spinning round and round on the grill of hell. Pigs lived through any possible torture humans had imagined in their future hell every day around lunch and dinnertime. Teeth devouring bites of flesh, destroying any leftovers that marked their existence on Earth. Thousands of living beings were reduced to calories – to the fat people ingested then hoped to lose weight for the summer.

The captain's laments were excruciating. Marxim held him tighter and tighter till they both wept, till his shirt was soaked in the hero's tears.

'They promoted these images, these trends on the 2018 people. Why? I think I can give you two reasons:

In 2018, as Russia cuts gas to Europe, they need a fast solution for the coming winters. Renewable energy isn't enough. They need another way to raise temperatures quickly.

'The meat industry was believed to be one of the world's causes for climate change. Increasing meat production in such a short time would have caused the fastest environmental 'damage' that, in this case, would have actually helped Europe, cutting its dependence on Russia's natural gasses. The result of the implementation of the meat industry? Hot rains, no more winters, no need for gas.'

'Yes, but why pigs? Why not chickens or cows? Cows are bigger.'

'Well, now it gets stranger. Let me show you these private documents I found. No, shit. Don't look, please don't look.'

But it was too late; Marxim burst out laughing at the pictures of a semi-naked Chekhovich posing for his alonenomore.com page.

'I bet the ladies go crazy for that ass. Oh, the boys too. Sorry, I didn't mean to be non-inclusive.'

'That was not … you were not meant to see that.'

But they kept laughing. The captain's laugh sounded like someone was slitting his throat.

'You should really upgrade your mind searcher,' Marxim advised.

'Gentlemen,' Chekhovich raised his voice.

'Men should dread fame like pigs dread being fat. As the fattest pig will be the first to be grilled, the man who doesn't dread fame will be the first to be killed.'

'What?'

Chekhovich cleared his voice:

'When after the clouds you'll call it home, a new god will rise to tame all the crowds. Not to be adored inside of a dome. Not to be controlled for money or gold.

He won't speak the language, but he'll show you the way.

Not all evolutions are considered progressions. Do not kill a chicken to teach monkeys a lesson.'

'What's that? There was no rhyme to it. I think you should leave spoken poetry to … literally anyone else. What did that even mean?'

'I didn't write this. It's a prophecy, I think. They found it during the demolition of the Great Wall of China to make the new loft area for the rising of Fantasity, the city of desires.'

The iridescent colours of the city shone on the hero's face. Buildings of violet and blue shades rose on the wall. A recorded voice narrated, 'The Fantasity Lofts offer an exciting opportunity to invest in the transformation of one of China's heritage attractions into cutting edge, twenty-third-century living space. It is located less than a five-minute walk from the Fantasity City – a thriving cosmopolitan city built upon a historical legacy and the centre of the economic Asian powerhouse.' A girl swimming in the pink waters of a lake invited the viewers to join her. The recorded voice continued, 'Our Pleasure Parks in Manson Street are located in the new historic Old Wall neighbourhood. It is currently undergoing an exciting regeneration as the last area to be de-naturalised and reinvigorated in the city centre with huge scope for capital appreciation.' A girl winked and threw her towel at the camera, and the screen burnt to black.

Printed on white letters was a last plea to potential buyers, 'Fantasity is rising to be a world-leading economy. Las Vegas economists predict that enjoyment growth in the city over the next five years will exceed many international capitals, including Paris, Amsterdam, and Prague.'

'How do you know all of this?'

'I have access to A'lex's news, the major news producer since … ever, I guess. Hear me now: 2017 was the year they discovered the first Earth-sized planet, *Home*. In the Chinese zodiac, that was the year of the rooster, and look here,' Chekhovich moved his finger, zooming in on the prophecy, 'Do not kill a chicken to teach monkeys a lesson.' They thought the modern God would be a chicken, so they created this trend of culinary destruction. Every restaurant that wanted to sell had to have chicken. Anybody who wanted to be somebody had to indulge in this trend. They targeted gym junkies mostly. Look at these meal preps: broccoli on chicken, rice on chicken, chicken on turkey, chicken on chicken …' Chekhovich paused and then continued, 'But then back in 2019, they discovered the second Earth-sized planet, *Home 2.0*, and it was the year of the pig in the Chinese Zodiac. So, they tried to exterminate them all as they did with the roosters. They were scared the prophecy might have come true.'

Chekhovich kneeled in front of the captain, holding his face in his arms. 'But you are alive. A little miracle.'

The captain's eyes sparkled, and he let Chekhovich pet him.

'Little? More like two tons of a miracle!' added Marxim.

'I am sorry I wrote that piece; A'lex commissioned it. But, you know, writing is the only thing I can do, and the only way you can write is with A'lex.'

'He forgives you,' said Marxim's yellow face.

'How do you know?' Chekhovich was both impressed and jealous of him.

'Telepathy, I guess.' Marxim shrugged. 'But I gotta say, your little story sounds a bit farfetched. Prophecy, economy – it all sounds very fanfictiony. I mean, how long did it take you to find this information? You do ten minutes of research and wanna write the whole book. Where did you find this information? How true can it be if it is available to anyone?'

'I am not anyone. I am ... I think it's time we see A'lex.'

Captain Grunter loaded his hoofs again, his eyes turning green.

***

With muzak in the background and dung under their soles (Captain Grunter had an accident when landing), the triumvirate of the father, the pork, and the spirited writer entered the concrete fortress where the truths of the world were raped, lobotomised, and rendered tolerable to the public. The inside of the building had the colours of an old movie theatre and the soul of a modern art gallery. Warm shades of red covered the interior of the lobby. Countless empty sofas and tables waited, white and hopeless, for a never-coming horde of guests on the left. In the cavernous space left between one sofa and another lay the conspicuous ostentation of wealth.

'We are here to see Mr A'lex,' said Chekhov to the receptionist who sat on a pedestal behind the desk. He could barely see the guests' faces.

'Do you have an appointment? No? Let me see what I can do. Yes, I can tell you to come back when you do have an appointment,' said the receptionist, looking at Marxim's dungaree with disdain.

'This is really not what I had in mind,' whispered Marxim to him. 'Just tell him Captain Grunter wants to personally thank A'lex—'

The receptionist suddenly got off his chair and slapped his legs in disbelief. 'Grunter, you said? Ah! Why didn't you say that before? Follow me. I am such a huge fan. I have all your posters, all your shirts. I even have a mould of your hoofprints!' Continuing the unstoppable flux of worthless adulation, the receptionist left the lobby unattended and led the guests through a red velvet corridor that ended in front of a diamond-shaped lift. A hundred floors up, the group arrived in front of the five-metre-high red and golden arabesque-covered door that secluded A'lex from the rest of the rabble. The receptionist hesitated before knocking.

'I am sure he will be thrilled to see you.' He opened the door wide. In the spacious room, everything was red: the floor, walls, chairs, tables, paintings, and lamps – it was all painted red. In the middle of the red room, A'lex's white suit shimmered. Without lifting his eyes from *The Comfort of Meat*, the paper he was reading, he addressed the intruders.

'I was wondering when you'd come to meet me,' A'lex said, snapping his fingers at the receptionist, who was uncertain if he was to step in or leave.

'Excuse the idiot; he's new. It's such a pleasure to finally meet you, Mr Captain, and you, Chekhovich. I hope you enjoyed writing your *last* piece.'

'Cut the crap, A'lex. We are here to talk about 2019,' Chekhovich demanded.

A'lex ran his hand through his slick and slightly green hair, an effect only achieved with original avocado oil, which was impossible to get nowadays. His features were confusing: sneaky little blue eyes framed by long and dark eyelashes, soft skin, a button nose, and finally, his lips, which his tongue constantly licked. His mouth was meaty and red from his bacon-flavoured lip balm, which he constantly over-applied. The most expensive sculptor in LA chiselled his jawline. The mix of babyish and evil features created confusion for anyone who looked at him.

A'lex walked around stomping his feet and spreading his metallic scent everywhere. His cologne was money and patchouli, a mix of privilege and armpit. A'lex scrutinised the guests: Marxim's ripped dungaree, Chekhovich's shit-stained shoes, and the captain's hoofs.

'Yes, my dears, such dreadful events, second only to the Avocado War.' A'lex licked his bacon-flavoured lips like an addict, throwing a whiff at Marxim and Chekhovich, who promptly licked their lips as well.

'And to the Chickenocide of 2017,' Chekhovich interrupted, waking up from the bacon spell he almost fell for.

'Yes, of course, as you know, Chekhovich, that was the atrocious result of an uncivilised culture,' said A'lex condescendingly as he applied more of his lip balm.

'I have been looking into it, and I couldn't find any news about the Chickenocide, only something in a 'Gazette Gazelle' of 2016. So, I was wondering if we could use your …'

'Say no more, Chekhovich. Captain Grunter's friends are my friends.' A'lex snapped his fingers, and the receptionist, who had been waiting behind the door just in case, entered.

'Hello, garbage, please show the gentlemen the mind records from 2015 to 2017.'

'2015 to 2017.'

'Yes, 2015 to 2017.'

'Follow me, please,' the receptionist said as he kept whispering, '2015 to 2017—2015 to 2017,' all while trying to stop his eye from twitching.

As the triumvirate walked towards the door, A'lex's docile voice interrupted the march.

'Actually, Captain, if you don't mind, I would love to talk to you in private.' He applied another thick layer of his lip balm.

The smell of bacon delighted the captain, who ignored the deadly nature of the scent. He looked at Marxim, who turned to look at Chekhovich, who looked at the pig. Everything was fine.

Just before the guests exited the room, A'lex snapped his fingers at the hesitant receptionist again.

'You know what to do,' A'lex said, smacking his lips.

His sinister whisper echoed in the room.

* * *

During the whole walk through the corridors, the stairs, and the various annexes, which brought them to the intestines of the building, the receptionist kept thinking about what A'lex told him, *'You know what to do.'* But did he? He lived his whole life by inertia. He woke up in the morning because his roommate had a loud alarm clock. He ate his mother's food first, then his girlfriend's, and then his roommate cooked for him. He got this receptionist job because he just entered the building after seeing the empty seat at the desk one day. He sat there to charge his mind recorder quickly, then one thing led to another, and he began buying stuff online, checking social media, and even scrolling through the news without really reading anything. After a couple of hours, he left his seat to look for a toilet, and instead, he found a huge woman screaming at him about how he knew it was unacceptable to wear glitter on a Wednesday and leave reception unattended.

She took him to HR to talk about his behaviour. Unfortunately, HR couldn't find any record of his employment. They apologised to the receptionist for losing such important documents, then immediately made new ones that officially made him part of A'lex's team.

'And this, gentlemen, is the majestic Mind Records Room. If you look on your right, you will see a map that will help you find your way through the years.' Chekhovich carefully wrote down every turn, every step, and every light they were passing while walking.

'Here is what you wanted to see, 2013-2022.'

'2015-20-' Marxim tried correcting the forgetful receptionist, but Chekhovich interrupted him.

'Yes, thank you.' He looked at Marxim and shrugged his shoulders; some extra years of knowledge couldn't hurt.

Marxim suspiciously stared at the receptionist, following every step he took, any movement his twitchy eyes made.

Chekhovich started his quest by roaming the corridors where seemingly empty shelving units followed each other into endless rows. Minuscule memory cards kept in see-through cases laid on the dusty shelves. The records didn't have names, only different formats (F1, F2, F3 …). The thought of decoding this recording system excited Chekhovich, but before he'd access any mind record, he would cruise through the much older, much more trustworthy paper printed documentation.

'Where can I find newspapers? Pictures? Essays? Anything organic at all?'

'Unfortunately, they destroy unused resources after ten years, I think.' Staring again at the dungaree, he whispered, 'But we do have A'lex's original mind record, somewhere around the department, in theory at least. 'It's probably gonna take some time to get them, but I might …'

Chekhovich sighed in despair; getting A'lex's mind record was a gamble. Swiftly, Marxim pushed the receptionist to the wall, and with a hand around his neck, he lifted the poor part-timer.

'Stop! What are you doing? Are you crazy, Marxim? Stop!' Chekhovich was clearly confused by Marxim's approach.

'What game are you playing? Where are these records?'

Chekhovich didn't know what to do. He didn't know Marxim much, but why would such an old ginger man be so aggressive?

'This is just a diversion, isn't it? What did A'lex mean by 'take care of them'?'

'He ... No, he didn't say that!'

'Oh, whatever. "You know what do to." What did he mean by that? I saw you nodding at him. What is it you have to do? You are just a decoy, aren't you?'

The receptionist could barely breathe, and for a second, his eyeballs were completely white. Marxim knew he had to stop if he didn't want to spend the rest of the day listening to Captain Grunter's disappointed and judgemental grunts. Marxim's hand released the receptionist, who fell onto the floor unconscious. Chekhovich was still bewildered and decided it was best to shut up and step back before Marxim's rage ran him over.

A slap echoed in the Mind Records Room. 'Tell me what he meant.'

Surrounded, the receptionist desperately tried to keep his eyes closed. But soon, the treacherous light blue eyes came back to life.

Chekhovich cleared his voice, 'Come on, mate, let's end this charade. Just tell us what you know.'

Blond curls bounced on his cheek, now wet with tears. He sat up, leaning on to the wall with his eyes still closed.

'What is it you had to do to us?' Marxim asked while loading another of his powerful slaps.

The receptionist cried, 'I have no idea, I swear! I just pretended to know. I never know what he means. I always pretend, and now you are gonna kill me ...'

'I don't believe you. Tell us the truth! Why did you take us here? You are just trying to hold us back, so A'lex has his time with the captain!'

'No, I swear. You have to believe me!'

'So, why did you take us on this endless tour?'

'Because …'

'Because …?'

'Because I'm new! I don't even know my way around here. That's why we have been walking so much. I swear I just started on Monday. Please don't kill me, please.'

'Tell us where A'lex's mind records are.'

'You are gonna kill me … A'lex is gonna kill me … Everybody is gonna kill me!'

'Just tell us what we want to know, and we will let you go. I swear nobody cares about you.'

'But I don't know! I really don't. I am just part-time here.'

The receptionist curled into a foetal position, and crying, added, 'It's a zero-hour contract.'

'What a cheap bastard. We must go back to A'lex's office immediately.'

* * *

Meanwhile, in the red room, A'lex smiled at the superhero. 'Would you like to get more comfortable, Captain Grunter? You look tired.'

Captain Grunter was tired of waiting, tired of being gentle, and he was also starving. He wanted the truth, and he wanted it that very moment, along with some pumpkin and carobs.

In the Red Room, Kyrie in D minor was echoing, creating the perfect atmosphere for the survival of the fittest.

'I guess you've had enough of this stupid game.'

The captain grunted sharply; his eyes turned green, and his hoofs came out.

'Before we start, I should thank Chekhovich.' He was now inspecting his teeth in a small mirror. 'Without him, you wouldn't be here now.' He licked his teeth and briskly closed his pocket mirror. 'For being a superhero, you don't ask many questions,' A'lex added, 'but it's understandable. Just like the rest of the population, you don't get paid to think, and why would you? No, you are a swine of action.'

The captain's eyes were still green. He was ready to strike, his hoofs poised for attack.

'Well, let's get to know each other. How's your family? Nice and shat for years now, I imagine. Yes, very sad,' A'lex said while walking around the room. 'I also had a lonely childhood. That's why my lovely parents adopted a little one to play with me. How sweet she was, my little Becky! Well, *sweet and sour*. She was so cute with that black spot on her nose, her lazy eye, and her limp.'

The captain's war grunts, which before had been thundering, suddenly stopped.

'Well, she wasn't always limping, of course not, but after we cut off her ham, she was never the same.'

Terror and tears gushed from the eyes of the hero as he collapsed on the floor.

'There, there, piggy. Come on, be a man! What if I'd told you your sister is here?' A'lex snapped his fingers. 'Come on, cheer up, Captain. Guys, bring Becky in.'

The captain's eyes turned brown and human, and for one second, a glimpse of hope and forgiveness beat in the pig's chest.

A parade of waiters marching like soldiers entered the room, holding trays they left on the million-dollar bonsai desk. Each tray was covered with a metal lid. However, the captain was still waiting for the triumphal entry of his long-lost sister. A'lex invited the captain to come much closer. A delicious smell pervaded the room.

'I must ask you, was Becky short for Rebecca or …' Then, in succession, the waiters raised the lids and left the room.

They revealed sausages, bacon slices, steaks, and at the centre, an Italian spit-roasted pig adorned with Ray-Ban aviator sunglasses and a lemon in its mouth.

'Or is Becky short for Bacon?' A'lex added.

The lights started flickering. The captain cried in spasms so strong, the tiles of the pavement moved. A'lex's smile lightened the immensity of the crimson room, and he drew a gun from his pocket.

'Any last oink before dinner?'

In the meantime, Marxim and Chekhovich rushed to the Red Room after the Mind Records flop and arrived to see the final scene of the hero saga.

A'lex opened fire.

'Captain!' shouted Marxim as he jumped in front of him. The bullet caught him in the calf. Hearing Papá Marxim's yells, the super pig woke up. The captain screamed, letting out an energetic wave that immobilised A'lex, forcing him down to his knees.

Once again, Chekhovich felt superfluous. He was never brave and, unfortunately, not stupid enough to jump in front of a bullet. He just stood there, watching and feeling incompetent.

The captain was levitating, his eyes were completely green, and the sinister expression on his face made him look once again more almost human.

A'lex nervously giggled until he couldn't move his lips anymore. Then, as he tried to utter his last words, distorted sounds came out of his mouth. After that, he did not have lips anymore, nor hands, nor feet. Marxim and Chekhovich, shocked at the sight of the bloody remains of A'lex's bones and clothes, vomited. Captain Grunter promptly rushed to eat up the hot mess.

A curly tail appeared between the shreds of A'lex's white suit, and a sad baby grunt accompanied the reborn A'lex, who, though shy and uncertain, took his first steps as a swine.

'Captain, are you alright?' said Marxim worriedly as he held his wound oozing with a thick red matter. He tried to pat Captain Grunter, but his rind became covered with painful blisters as his stained hand touched the pig. The Captain immediately ran off and rubbed his back on the nearby couch, squealing in pain. Marxim smelled his hand. What A'lex fired was evidently a barbecue sauce bullet. 'What a sick bastard,' he said, licking his fingers.

Grunting and crying, A'lex tried to escape, but Chekhov, green and red in the face, ran behind the little pig and managed to grab him by his tail.

'You are gonna tell us everything now. Let's start from the beginning.'

'Maria! Stop writing,' the man shouted. 'Come back outside. It's time for the second drip irrigation.'

'I have no… I haven't drunk in days! I have no pee left.'

Maria looked like she could have died any second.

'Maybe if you didn't cry so much, we would have more. Now, where is the emergency bottle?'

'We used it on Wednesday, remember?'

'But for sure, there's some left. I wouldn't have just…'

'Oh, you are right. It was only 100.5 ml, and I gave it to Tonia for her baby.'

A smack echoed in the room, burning on Maria's cheek.

A tear appeared in Captain Grunter's green eyes. He always hated to see the innocent suffer, even if it was just a far image from somebody else's memory.

Loosening the grip on A'lex's ear, the captain interrupted the mind-reading session while the other pig oinked in pain, rushing to hide behind the red velvet curtain. Then, giving one last green-eyed look at his crowd, the captain fainted. When he woke up, his eyes were brown again.

'What have you seen?' asked Chekhovich, slapping the captain's rind.

'Let him breathe, for Manson's sake!' pleaded Marxim, pushing Chekhovich back.

Using telepathy, the captain showed them the memory he had extracted from A'lex.

After they watched it silently, Marxim patted the captain's ears, and Chekhovich turned A'lex's mind searcher on. Chekhovich loved mind searchers; he couldn't even imagine what life was like before the invention of this small purple disk, capable of containing people's entire internet chronology and electronic files. He loved to think that it was the invention of the decade because all Starbucks had closed, and there was no point in carrying a laptop around anyway.

Eager to try something new – multitasking – he started to speak nervously, rushing his words. 'Capitan, we have to go back into A'lex's head. We need to know more about it. We need to know why they invested so much in the avocado plantations and why the Bacon Wave? We need to know the why of everything!'

'Give him a break. We'll end up frying him. He's just a pig.'

Noticing the broken piggy pride in the captain's low gaze, Marxim apologised. 'No. I didn't mean it like that. You are a magnificent specimen, an elevated soul, and you know it.'

Flattered, the captain oinked, dramatically moving his head and sinuously sashaying towards A'lex, his fellow pig, a troubled pig, a pig who had not yet accepted his transformation from A'lex, CEO of A'lex News — the one and only news producer since 2016; to A'lex, the novice pig. The new A'lex looked at his hoofs with contempt, even though he had always shown a natural talent for *swinery* throughout his career.

A'lex and the captain exchanged long looks of repulsion. It was a faceoff between an animal who wanted to be more than a walking plate of pork chops and a man who wanted nothing more than asserting his superiority by attacking the same pork chops with knife and fork. Soon, the pigs started a conversation in piggish. A'lex kept making mistakes, but the captain pretended not to notice. That's the kind of pig he was: gentle, understanding, pink. A pig who noticed everything but kept his muzzle shut. A pig who didn't laugh at the sight of the timid bump appearing between Chekhovich's legs, the two inches of genuine excitement for the avalanche of news that was about to come. A small light from the mind searcher projected the results on a white wall, and Chekhovich stood there, lost between his awe and disgust about the series of newspaper titles that started to appear:

'STRONTSKY CUTS OFF GAS SUPPLIES TO EUROPE. ENCLOSED THE PICTURES OF HIS ADORABLE PUPPIES IN MINK FUR.'

'EUROPE DOOMED. COUNTDOWN TO THE BIG FREEZE. THE ULTIMATE

BUCKET LIST: THINGS TO DO
BEFORE FREEZING TO DEATH.'

'HOPE AT LAST. MANSON LAUNCHES
"FARTING FOR EUROPE." THE ANIMALS
THAT ARE SAVING OUR COUNTRIES.'

'DINE IN: BREASTS OUT! TOP 10 CHICKEN
RECIPES FOR KEEPING WARM THIS WINTER.'

'IT'S CHICKEN O'CLOCK! ORDER THIS
AT THE RESTAURANT, AND NOBODY
WILL EVER CALL YOU RATCHET.'

'CHICKENOCIDE? WE ONLY CALL IT DINNER!
CARNIVORE MANIFESTO ENCLOSED.'

'SOME WEAR IT, SOME EAT IT.
BACON WAVE HITS THE UK.'

'MANSON TAKES CONTROL OF CLIMATE
CHANGE. WINTERS CANCELLED TILL 2090.'

'BYE-BYE BACON: MILLIONS IN
TEARS AS FACTORIES ANNOUNCE
INTERRUPTED PRODUCTION.'

The titles brightened up the room and the young face of the journalist. Imagining he was the Bob Woodward of his century, he nodded, pretending to make sense of things.

'MOST LIKELY TO BE FLOODED IN 2033.
IS YOUR COUNTRY ON THE LIST?'

'HOT OR NOT? SEA LEVEL RISE? WHO
CARES? GET YOUR BODY BEACH-READY.'

'THIS FRUIT INCREASES MENTAL
AND PHYSICAL PRODUCTIVITY.
YOU'LL NEVER GO BACK.'

'THE NEW CHIC: THIS RESTAURANT
MAKES EVERYTHING AVOCADO'ED!'

'SCANDAL: THEY LOOK LIKE YOU, BUT THEY
ARE TRAITORS. MEET THE U.K. FAMILIES
WHO HIDE PIGS FROM THE NATION.'

'JUSTICE IS RESTORED: PIG-HIDING
FARMERS EXECUTED AND HIDDEN PIGS
TURNED TO BACON. WILL YOU BE THE
ONE WHO GETS THE LAST PACK?'

'TO EAT OR NOT TO EAT? THE ETHICAL
CHOICE OF AVOCADOS'- CANCELLED

'THE RIPEST AVOCADOS? GET YOUR
OWN. GRAB A GIFT VOUCHER FOR
A TRIP TO SOUTH AMERICA!'

'THE BLACK MARKET OF AVOCADOS,
YOU WILL NEVER IMAGINE WHO'S
CONTROLLING IT.'- CANCELLED

'FARMERS STRIKE IN BOLIVIA. MEET
THE DISSIDENTS.'- CANCELLED

'YOU TOLERATED THEM BEFORE; YOU HATE THEM NOW: BOLIVIAN FARMERS MASSACRE U.K. AVOCADO TOURISTS (WITH PICTURES).'

'STATE FUNERALS FOR THE AVOCADO VICTIMS: OUR DEAREST PRESIDENT MANSON WEARS PURPLE TUXEDO.'

'MANSONISM: AS EASY AS IT SOUNDS. THE 1 STEP GUIDE TO RESPECT THE VICTIMS FOR FIFTY YEARS (IN SILENCE).'

'THE BALLS TO BREAK MANSONISM: REPORTERS GONE MISSING.' - CANCELLED

'SURVIVOR OF SWINE GENOCIDE MEETS WORLD.' - CANCELLED

'IT'S BACON; IT FLIES; IT READS YOUR MIND: CAPTAIN GRUNTER, LAST OF THE PIGS AND FIRST OF THE HEROES.'

Shivers ran through Chekhovich's spine; it was exciting. But it was also scary, and his frightened armpits stained his grey shirt with sweat. He knew he was entering a dangerous path – a dangerously heated, sticky, and smelly path. To make it worse, the hot rain bashing on the windows increased the room temperature, and the steam blurred the images on the wall. Chekhovich felt deeply uncomfortable. The delicious smell of flesh and limbs on the desk was debilitating him.

'Marxim! I need a break. Maybe we can transfer everything to my mind searcher and head back to the farm. Marxim!'

Not hearing a response, Chekhovich walked towards Marxim, who was sleeping on a luxurious red velvet armchair. As the young man tried to wake up the old, he heard a rumble of thunder as what seemed to be a girl entered the room. Chekhovich immediately turned off the mind searcher while, in a secretarial and professional tone, the girl called A'lex's name. She was pretty but also pretty short. She had long, wavy brown hair, freckles, and clearly not a lot of patience.

'A'lex, where a–'

She stopped, finally noticing the two men next to the talky-talky section. Her eyes went from the man who was standing, young and moderately handsome, to the other, barely awake and looking like he belonged in a morgue.

'Who are you? What are you doing in A'lex's office?' The girl held her index finger up, ready to press the yellow button on the alarm pen she wielded in Chekhovich's face. A'lex oinked loudly and rushed towards the girl while shreds of fabric hung from his tail.

Marxim tried to explain, 'Look, lady, we are here with Mister Grunter. We are …'

'What! No way.' She kneeled to the wrong pig and started stroking his ears. 'Shut up! Captain Grunter? It's such a pleasure to meet you, Captain Grunter. You are my hero!'

A'lex bit the hand of the girl.

'I guess someone doesn't like cuddles,' she whispered, retracting her hand. 'Asshole.'

'I always imagined him bigger and cuter.' The girl was now looking at the pig in disgust.

'As a matter of fact, he is. Look, this is Captain.'

Marxim intervened, pointing at the more majestic pig.

Captain Grunter tip-tapped his hoofs on the floor impatiently to get his much-deserved praise and attention. The captain had the look and grace of a Large White and the charm of a wild boar. He was long bodied with excellent hams and fine white hair. He had warrior hoofs and big brown eyes, erect ears, and a perfectly curled tail. He bowed elegantly to the girl.

'The one you were playing with is–' Marxim was interrupted by Chekhovich.

'It's really not important. But look, lady, you should go. We have important matters to discuss with A'lex.'

'Aw, no way. Look at those eyes!'

The captain posed, flexing his butt muscles and lighting his eyes to impress the woman.

Chekhovich grabbed the girl by her arm. 'Please, lady, you should really–'

'Don't touch me! You are not my boss.'

She calmly adjusted her turtleneck and cleared her throat. 'You should not be in the office while A'lex is not here.'

'But he is.' Marxim's words were soon followed by a cry as Chekhovich pinched him.

'Excuse me? Should I believe you or my own eyes?

There's no one else who–'

'Look down, lady,' said Marxim.

A'lex shook his curly tail and oinked, munching on the girl's trousers. She jumped back, screaming.

'No way! What is this? You turned him into a pig?'

'Keep it down. I am sure it's reversible.'

'Reversible?' The girl laughed hysterically. 'I really hope not.' She started to kick A'lex in the stomach. 'It suits him. But no offence, Mr Grunter, because you totally are my hero.'

Captain Grunter grunted, flattered. He loved being a hero just as much as he loved being called a hero or rolling in his own shit. He looked at the girl as if waiting for something. With her breath still laboured from all the kicking, she fixed her trousers and cleared her throat. 'My name is Lucretia. I am A'lex's personal ass—'

'Excuse me, I don't mean to be rude, but your name tag says Stupid Slave?' Chekhovich's interruption was more like a whisper. He was obviously scared of her.

Lucretia threw another kick at A'lex, who ran behind Marxim as she explained, 'Oh well, what can I say? That's just … banter, right?'

She took her name tag off and, chasing A'lex, tried to poke him with it.

'Come here, little piggy,' her voice echoed in the large room.

Trying to stop her, Marxim decided to introduce himself.

'Lucretia dear, nice to meet you. I am Marxim, and this is …'

'Chekov Chekhovich. I know it may sound familiar, I'm actually a colleague.'

Lucretia stopped tormenting A'lex and looked at Chekhovich from top to bottom. 'Oh yes, I believe I read a couple of your articles, but you've got a bit of a shitty first name, isn't it Ceko? Quite repetitive, just like your articles.'

Chekhovich's face turned red while Marxim tried to change the subject. 'Dear, tell me, should we expect more guests?'

Holding her index to her temple, she connected to the timetabling team. 'Hey hun, clear the whole afternoon. Yes, I am sending you the new schedule. Yes, yes, until Monday, everything's off. He ate cheese again. Yes … disgusting!' Lucretia winked at Marxim, 'Bye, hun. Yes, drinks on me tomorrow. Yes, yes … Bye … yes. Bye … yes, bye.'

The hot storm outside stopped, and a fresh breeze came through one of the open windows, hitting Chekhovich on his sweaty neck. Lucretia looked at him and began her attack with relentless questions.

'So, what are you doing here?' Lucretia asked with her stripper self-confidence and hooker drive.

'Well, we came to talk to A'lex, but things got out of hand.'

'And you turned him into a pig?' Lucretia was not afraid of asking uncomfortable questions, and why would she, after all? Nobody listened to women anyway.

'Clearly, but that wasn't the plan.'

'So, what now?'

'We want to go through his mind searcher so we can learn–'

'What? Learn history?'

'Yes?' Chekhovich shrugged his shoulders.

'And what's the point? People never learn from history. That's why they are going to cancel the Rwandan genocide from the cyber school program.'

'That's ridiculous. Our dearest President Manson is never going to approve that. People actually enjoy learning history.'

'Learning history? Maybe, but learning from history? That's just a myth.'

Lucretia moved the bacon tray and bit her lips as she gazed at the liquid gold grease. She sat on the million-dollar bonsai desk, ready to offer her opinion. 'Hear me out, I had this friend, right. She had a boyfriend, and he cheated. He gave her gonorrhoea, she cried, he cried, and they broke up. Then after a couple of years, they started talking again. They went on a date, and they slept together. You'd think she had learnt her lesson, right?' She nodded to the men, who looked baffled, 'Like, have sex with a damn condom, right? But no, she didn't. She got HIV and never got tested. Bitch is dead now.'

'Your point?'

'History always repeats itself.'

'Can we go back to … wait, where were we?'

Chekhovich was lost.

'You didn't download all the content of the mind searcher, right?'

'No, but …'

Lucretia snatched the purple mind searcher from his hands, operating it with confidence. She knew exactly where to look and squinched quite a lot, zooming in and out of documents and folders.

'What year are you interested in? Never mind. I'll get everything.'

She pressed her finger on one of the buttons and transferred all the material to her device.

'No, wait! Why did you do that? Why on your memory?'

'What's this pout for?' asked Lucretia, as if speaking to a child. 'Don't you know that downloading information to any device not cleared for corporate memory access sends a signal to the police? Don't you know that?' She pinched Chekhovich's cheek. He was no longer the Bob Woodward of his century but the silly boy who gets his lunch stolen at school.

'Yes, now smile, pretty boy.' She modelled a smile on his face.

'Leave me alone, you b–'

'Excuse me? Did you just try to call me a bitch?' Lucretia acted enraged.

'What's the big deal? You just called your friend that.'

'I am a woman; women can call each other that.'

'Just apologise, Ceko,' Marxim interrupted them.

'She's got a point.'

'I am sorry for calling you a stupid bitch.'

'But you didn't call her stupid,' Marxim whispered to his ear.

'OK, Marxim, why don't you get these pigs something to eat? I can help Ceko here,' Lucretia said, checking out the pork feast behind her.

Marxim agreed, looking at the pigs with fatherly pride. He was relieved. The captain finally had the chance to interact with someone from his species after Marxim stole the opportunity from him. The captain rushed towards him shaking his tail while A'lex protested, sounding just like a pig entering the slaughterhouse. After a bit of running around and sweet-talking, he finally surrendered and let Marxim pick him up. He was so tired that he even let Lucretia pet and insult him.

'Be good,' Marxim winked to Chekhovich. 'Nice to meet you, milady.' He kissed Lucretia's hand and jumped on Captain Grunter's back. Marxim held the former villain tight as they flew home, and they disappeared into the lilac sky dressed up in stars.

Wishing for A'lex to fall from Marxim's arms and hit the ground and then be run over by a bus, Lucretia sat again on the million-dollar bonsai desk. Chekhovich knew this was the right moment to act.

'OK, tell me everything you know about A'lex and his corporation.'

'Oh, my Manson, chill. Get a drink, let's eat some food. You look like you could use some food. Poverty is so 2020. When was the last time you had pork?'

'I just want to get everything I need and get out of here.'

'But why?' She took off her shoes. 'Let me fix you a drink.'

'Actually … no, why are you even helping me? What's your motive?'

'My motive?' She sauntered towards the corner of the office to a bar that could serve the needs of hundreds of guests. Between the excitement and the commotion, Chekhovich had not even noticed it.

'I guess I like Mondays.' Lucretia went through all the forty bottles of spirits that sat on the black granite countertop.

'Today is Wednesday.'

'Look, whatever, I am bored and willing. What's wrong with that? Isn't that your type anyway?' Looking for something more expensive, Lucretia marched towards the backdrop of the bar, where countless dark bottles added another layer of sophistication to the room. The LED backlighting, which changed according to the guest's mood, was now pink. But neither Lucretia nor Chekhovich knew it, so they still acted as if they hated each other.

Maybe it was a shiver of desire, perhaps just fear, but Chekhovich suddenly winced.

'What? Are you scared of someone coming in? Well, you should be more afraid of me spitting in your drink.' She handed him a cherry Scotch on the rocks, enjoying his hesitation.

'The building will be empty in just three minutes.'

Chekhovich looked confused but didn't ask for explanations. Instead, he went back to sipping his drink, wishing he could hold it in his mouth forever.

'Only poor people work after five. Obviously.'

Chekhovich was one of those poor people. He knew nothing of the world Lucretia was talking about, and the spirit he was drinking was worth more than his life. He spent everything he earned on rent, second-hand patent shoes, and food.

Being around this opulence, he began to judge the squalor of his life. Of course, he could never be that rich, but maybe he could have a piece of that life. That's when he realised his blooming desire for Lucretia.

Chekhovich didn't want to lose sight of his intention and needed to concentrate on something serious – the decline of civilisation, his mother's suicide, the genocide of the animals, the increasing price of tofu, anything. He looked at Lucretia like a man who knows what he wants.

'So, do you mind talking about serious business now?'

'Two questions: are you going to pay me for my overtime? And what do you want to know?'

'Why? Do you know everything?'

'Not yet, but remember the download? I'll know almost everything A'lex knows. Every document he signed, every document he covered up, every girl and boy he stalked on the internet, which kind of dildos he prefers, what he ordered for dinner 247 days ago.'

'247 days ago?'

'His anniversary with what's her name, your mother?'

Chekhovich lowered his head as if admitting defeat, but Lucretia continued.

'Can't you take a joke? You are so sad.'

Lucretia was right, he was a sad individual. Everything about his looks confirmed that: his ironic moustache, long hair held in a man bun, and the padded pants he wore to enhance his masculinity.

'Cut the crap, Lucretia, just tell me everything you know already.'

'Why don't you tell me what you know?'

Finally having a chance to shine, Chekhovich started to explain. 'OK, starting from 2019 Russia cuts–'

'No, not Russia, my dear. Strontsky. Democracy is for the ancient Greeks and recent gays. Decisions are made by one, remember?'

'So Strontsky stops supplying gas to Europe and "Farting for Europe" looks like the only solution—a solution that is just too good for the palate of the citizens. So, when there are no more pigs and chickens left, people start talking about the dinnerocides: the Chickenocide and the Bacon Wave. In the general panic, the European leaders ...'

'Our dearest President Manson, not the European leaders. Decisions ...'

'Are made by one. So, our dearest President Manson has to deal with the emissions from the meat plants and the overwhelming temperature rise. Rather than blaming him, the media celebrates him as the hero of the moment with articles like "Manson takes control of climate change. Winters cancelled till 2090." Around 2023, while the winters are almost non-existent, meteorologists register storms of hot rains. Those who express their concerns about the rising sea level disappear. So, here comes another solution, this thing with the avocados, but I don't understand where it comes from.'

'Let me see ...' Lucretia opened one of the most recent downloads in her mind searcher and explained. 'Fine ... Because of the sea level thing, President Manson invests in avocado plantations in South America. I don't expect plebs like you to understand, but avocados are delicious, and they need lots of water to grow. So, they water the plantations with filtered ocean water. The avocado demand was so high that in places with no sea access, it was tragic. All the lakes had been drained, and rain had stopped falling. At least, this is what some journalists were saying before the Mansonism. It makes sense. It not only makes the sea level go down, but it also recycles developing countries.'

'Wow. Maybe you need a filter. Where is the Twitter Police when you need them?

'Whatever, I'm from one of those countries, so I can say it.'

'You sure are pretty stupid for someone in a suit.'

Lucretia jumped off the couch. Grabbing Chekhovich's neck from behind, she whispered, "Should I take it off?"

Chekhovich was nervous and started to think of all the online games he played and how they all finished with 'You lose. Next round? You lose.' He saw all the trains he missed because of the time he wasted looking at himself in the mirror, inspecting his nostrils for wild hair. He remembered his days as a pizza delivery guy, of all the doors closed in his pimply face before he even had the time to ask the customers if they wanted to try a complimentary glass of Caca-Cola. 'It's like Coca-Cola, but instead of burning your intestines, it helps your gastric flora.' He saw the face of his dad laughing at his ballet improvisations in the living room. He felt the awkwardness of his mother's goodbye kiss outside the school gates on the day she died. He regretted that moment every day, or most days, at least, when he remembered. Had he behaved differently, would his mother still have killed herself? Perhaps he wouldn't have ended up a full-time delivery guy and part-time journalist who mostly wrote junk articles and ads for dating sites. Maybe he wouldn't have been an emotional wreck, someone who second-guessed every decision he ever made in his life, from saying hello instead of good morning to not crying at his mother's funeral. To him, everything was equally unforgivable and wrong.

Had he behaved differently on that day, maybe he would have been able to grab Lucretia's hand and tell her to fuck off. Or grab her face and kiss her. He started thinking about all the possible scenarios: He'd kiss her, and she'd slap him, or what if he slapped her – would she kiss him? He was unsure of the etiquette in this case.

She walked back to the bar, leaving him there feeling guilty for what he wanted to do and guiltier for what he never did. With the confidence of the Pisa Tower, Chekhovich watched

Lucretia going through the poisons, hoping she hadn't noticed his interest in her. She turned to look at him and resumed the investigation.

'Honestly, you are so gay. Yes, Twitter Police, blah, blah – it's actually a compliment. But yes, going back to the avocado thing, it says that President Manson and his "friends" worked on this project.'

'Which friends?'

'I don't know; I am still downloading the memory. But I do remember reading some articles about it.' Lucretia sounded preoccupied. She was looking for Maraschino cherries, not for the truest of the truths.

'That's impossible. I would not have missed it. I read everything.'

'You can't read what was never printed ... what was never approved.'

'Right. The Manson Law. But I don't understand.'

'Where are the damn Maraschino cherries? Clearly not right next to the olives, as they should be.' Lucretia kept scavenging for luxuries that Chekhovich had never tasted. He went back to the timeline, hoping that Lucretia would stop making him feel so second class.

'I don't understand why they stopped at chickens and pigs. Why not cows? Why not ... sharks?'

'Obviously, cows are not as tasty as pigs. Plus, they already have a purpose: white Russians. And sharks, really? Their food is literally plastic.'

Still looking for the cherries, Lucretia hit a bottle of whisky, which fell on a bottle of cognac, which fell on a bottle of vodka, which fell on ten other bottles.

'Strike!' screamed Lucretia in awe.

Chekhovich left his cherry Scotch on the desk and got up to re-arrange the bottles in the order he thought made more sense: the Macallan, the Mendis, the Diva and the Pasión Azteca Platinum in the front, and the more bohemian spirits, like the Martel, the Imperial, and the Belvedere, in the back. Lucretia looked at him, annoyed. She didn't want to clean the mess; she wanted to drink it all, starting with the D'Amalfi Limoncello Supreme that he held in his hands.

'Do you know how much this cost? But, of course, you don't. You're like the Little Match Girl with a moustache. That would be £44.5 million.'

Now cautious to the extreme, Chekhovich placed the bottle next to the other jewels, relieved that he hadn't broken anything. He did not know why he still cared about keeping the place tidy. A'lex was gone.

'You are definitely cleaning my room tonight,' Lucretia told him, laughing while Chekhovich's usual sad expression turned into a grin of preoccupation.

'What is that?' he asked, horrified.

'What's wrong? It's really not a big deal. I usually take my dog out to relieve himself like at least once per week.'

'Shut up!' he shouted, pointing in the direction of a basic bottle of vodka. 'Absolut Vodka. What is that doing here?'

'Ah! This brings me back to like … my golden years. I remember when …'

'Why would A'lex keep a bottle of Absolut in his millionaire bar? Even I can afford that.'

'Sentimental value?' She cleared her throat.

'Maybe it reminds him of where he comes from and the struggles he had to face before becoming A'lex. Yes, it might be symbolic.'

'Oh, come on, the only struggle A'lex might have faced was the gold of his bidet being too cold in the morning.'

'What do you mean?'

'Well, rich people have bidets, so richer people must have gold bidets. I mean, why not? A'lex's father was Strontsky's uncle. You must have read about him ... the guy who cut off the gas supplies in 2017, no 16, no, whatever. It turns out that was only a marketing strategy. It's all here.' Lucretia pointed at her forehead while the light on A'lex's mind searcher showed that the download to her memory was still active.

Chekhovich lowered his head. He knew the news was *adjusted*, but he always hoped that if he kept reading everything available to the public, he might have found a little truth in the cauldron of lies and lesser lies. At this moment, with Lucretia, he felt betrayed by the world he had so desperately tried to be part of. A'lex's story, that of a humble call centre operator who built his empire one call at a time, was what put Chekhovich to sleep every night. He now felt ashamed for ever believing it.

Lucretia smiled at him again. 'You are so naïve. But I totally get you.'

Chekhovich looked confused.

'You know, like when your girlfriend, or boyfriend, or XXY partner is cheating on you, and you don't have the proof, but you can smell male, female, and gender-fluid fluids on them, and you don't say anything because you are doing worse. Then one day, probably the worst day of the week, your boss is like: "You're not hot enough to be so stupid. How can your ass be so fat yet so flat?" and so on. So, to feel better, you go back home with a huge pizza, right? No, because not only does that pizza that was supposed to make you feel better give you diarrhoea – because apparently, you are now gluten intolerant – but to top up this awful day, you add some haemorrhoids to the equation.'

Lucretia took a poignant pause and dried the theatrical tears from her eyes. 'You think it's over, right? No. I go home to find all my lovers together, naked on my bed doing things. Oh, and my dog is there watching. And that's like the worst because aren't dogs supposed to be your best friends?' Lucretia touched her chest as if to contain all her pain. 'But I had him castrated, so we are fine now,' she added, stealing the tissue Chekhovich had in his front pocket.

'The dog or ...'

'So, don't judge yourself too harshly. We are both so naïve.'

Lucretia shook her head and, grabbing the Absolut Vodka bottle, waved it in Chekhovich's face. As she moved it, Lucretia noticed that something was moving inside of it. She rushed to empty the content of the bottle in the sink but, as whatever she thought she had seen was still stuck inside, she shrugged and then smashed the bottle against the granite. Barehanded, she analysed every piece of glass until she found the mysterious something. Tiny fragments of glass shone on her right hand, but she didn't seem to care. She calmly washed away the crystals, squeezing what remained in her hand: a rubberised see-through key.

'What is that?'

Chekhovich couldn't hide his excitement, and his eyes now sparked with life, like those of a child getting their first iPad.

'A key? Yes. Do I know what it opens? Not really.'

Frantically, Chekhovich started to move the bottles, looking for a safe, or a box, or anything with a lock.

'I doubt anyone would keep a key so close to whatever it opens, hun. This is not the Purloined Letter.'

'You are right. Where then?'

'I guess we just have to wait for the download to finish. Maybe I'll have an address.'

Chekhovich looked at his watch nervously.

'Shouldn't we leave now? I guess the cleaners will come soon.'

'Chill, Ceko. A'lex likes his office cleaned in the morning; his lady comes at 5:00 a.m.'

* * *

Elsewhere in the building, the clanking of Italian leather shoes echoed across the corridors.

A big-chested man, whose Monaco suit retracted at every step, was walking towards A'lex's office. His look was impeccable: tailor-made jacket and ultra-skinny trousers, very generous on the crotch.

'I hear something,' Lucretia whispered, grabbing a bottle of Belvedere with one hand and Chekhovich with the other. She dragged him behind a couch, telling him to man up or shut up, and obviously, Chekhovich decided to shut up. After a few minutes, the man in the Monaco suit slowly walked to the desk, where Lucretia had left A'lex's mind searcher.

'Fuck! What's A'lex doing here?' Chekhovich whispered.

Lucretia stifled a laugh. 'That's definitely not him, hun. Look between his legs.'

'Why? I'm not gay … homosexual … homophile, yes.'

'Men of his power are genetically not well-hung. It's like one of the astrophysics laws. Plus, I've seen it. In a totally professional way, obviously.'

In the meantime, what looked exactly like A'lex started to speak in a mechanical, emotionless voice, examining the glass Chekhovich had left on the desk.

'Order-of-the-day. Approve-article-for-print. Desk-not-in-order. Remind-A'lex-to-check-security-cameras. Remind-Lucretia-she-is-a-stupid-stupid-stupid-fat-ugly-ass-fat-bitch. Fat.'

'Damn, I always wondered who did the job while A'lex was bored or like busy with me, but we should totally leave now.'

Lucretia crawled towards the door at the back of the office. Chekhovich followed her. The doppelganger kept recording vocal memos.

Outside the office, the two fought silently, alternating insults and pleas. Chekhovich wanted to stay and see which articles would be approved or discarded. Lucretia wanted to leave, worried that what looked like A'lex would have found out someone was downloading the content of A'lex's mind searcher.

'We have to go, hun. Now! I don't know if you've noticed or were too busy getting lost in your little world of cookies and cream, but that thing beeps like a bitch at every 10% of downloading. And I don't know about you, hun, but I'd like to keep my ass whole.'

Lucretia's last point seemed to finally convince Chekhovich, who forgot about his journalistic dreams and tiptoed outside the building following his new puppet master.

A'lex 2.0 received a new notification. He read it aloud.

'Download-interrupted. A'lex-1st-download-work-also- when-sick. What-a-great-guy-we-are.'

* * *

'Take off my panties.'

'What?'

'I said take my panties from the drawer and give them to me. Come on, Ceko, have you never packed in your life? We need clean underwear and passports.'

Chekhovich walked cluelessly, waiting for a hint or direction. The hint never came, and he had to use his super special detective superpowers. Finally, he saw a towel on the floor, where there's one, there's two … Jackpot. 'You said you were gonna tell me about the Manson Law for articles,' he said appalled, as he browsed the cabinet in the bathroom that carried the vast undies and old towels.

'Oh yeah, it's really not complicated. They run the articles through FinalFantasy, an algorithm that analyses the pieces according to their incomprehensibility, the number of hashtags they contain, and stuff like keyword density. Every article has a 3% allowance. Words like *Chickenocide, war, Bolivia, freedom,* and *Twitter Police* take that 3% allowance. More than that, and the article will not be published.'

'But then people can still find a way to write about these topics,' Chekhovich said, wielding a pair of black knickers. 'They just need to find other words.'

'People need repetition and clarity these days; you cannot beat around the bush. Plus, bushes are so late Feminism, and if they find you, they will kill you. Around 400 writers have already been silenced for Mansonism in the U.K. in less than ten years. Actually, I think that's how you got your job. OMG, Ceko, now I am gonna have a bitch fit. When I said panties, I didn't mean pants. Why do you think I'd want to bring these? Am I going away? Yes. Am I going to a convent? No.'

'They looked … comfortable.'

'These are my period panties,' Lucretia said, throwing her old underwear on the floor and packing her bag with sexy lingerie. 'Plus, Captain Grunter is going to be there.'

'Right. You realise he's a pig?'

'You realise he's my hero?'

Lucretia was deeply annoyed by his puritanism.

'Sure. Have you got anything to eat?'

'Check in the fridge; there might be some Chardonnay.'

Lucretia was clearly annoyed by his puritanism and sent him away. Looking for the kitchen, Chekhovich wandered around the apartment. It was a large and bright four-bedroom maisonette in Whitechapel, a place where the international hipsters would have gathered to discuss ground coffee and online lives in early 2020. A place they had all abandoned by 2025 when the increasing levels of carbon dioxide caused the sudden depopulation (by death or escape) of London. It was bad; the housing market collapsed, Chekhovich's father went bankrupt, and 'estate agent' became a job of the past, like ironmongery. But it was also good because the catastrophe restored London's demography, returning Whitechapel to its historical keepers: prostitutes and immigrants.

Once in Lucretia's kitchen, Chekhovich appreciated the dramatic effect of the chessboard tiles and the eye-popping red painted walls. He opened the fridge. A cold hint of onion smacked him on the right side of his face. But, like a good Christian, he turned the other cheek. His eyes scanned the probiotic yoghurt, raspberries, and an empty bottle of Chardonnay. It was as if you could tell an asshole lived in this house.

Lucretia called him. She wanted him to get a jumper from her room. She said her dog would lead the way, so Chekhovich followed Tom, Lucretia's castrated bastard, to what looked like a bit of heaven. The light blue walls were partly covered by candid white furniture and postcards of Istanbul, Damascus, and Naples, all before the revolts. Her window had no curtains, she was an exhibitionist, clearly, and her bedside drawers held a jar full of dry flowers, a pair of golden hoops, and two books, *For the Voice* by Mayakovski and *Damned* by Palahniuk. Chekhovich opened the drawer. Under a layer of socks, he found some wet wipes and a black dildo. Too curious for his own good, Chekhovich almost grabbed it to analyse its size, but Tom's low-pitched moans made him feel dirty. He then moved to the desk, a valley of dirty tissue and plastic wraps, and then towards the wardrobe. He opened it, wondering where he could have found the jumper Lucretia talked about in that mess of corsets, garments, latex dresses and pale pink dressing gowns with unicorn prints. Luckily, he found a few jumpers. Less luckily, he had to make yet another choice. One was black; one was of a pastel blue shade with ice cream cones jumping on clouds and stars. Another remarkable one had unicorns and prints saying: 'I always wake up cute.' He thought of choosing the latter but then predicted Lucretia's cackling complaints and opted for the safest option, as usual. He thought she would have preferred to look like a spy rather than a princess, at least this time. Somehow, Chekhovich had slowly started seeing Lucretia as a real person, someone with desires, fears, and predictable behaviours.

'Even bad bitches love unicorns, right, Tom?'

Tom's only response was a loud licking sound, so probably yes.

***

Downstairs, Chekhovich looked at Lucretia, smiling as if he knew a secret. Her unicorn passion made her more approachable. He sat down on a neon yellow chair and started to ask her questions.

'So, where are you from?'

'Why does it matter?' Lucretia was emptying boxes of dog food in various corners of the house. She wanted to keep Tom the dog, active.

'It does. It's who you are.'

Lucretia was annoyed.

'So, I am like war, desperation, sun, sea, and dirt, the screams of motherless children and the fury of the tanks.'

'I meant … I just wanted to make conversation.'

'Where I am from is where I am from, not who I am.'

'So, where is that?'

'A bit of everywhere. My father was from Damascus. After the first five years of the civil war, when he realised he could never win no matter the side he joined, he fled to Turkey. He said it was horrible, the kind of horrible that you'd expect people to do something about, but of course, nobody did; they just took pictures and made it a spectacle. So, in Istanbul, he was safe for a couple of years until the MF attacked Turkey and Lebanon. Again, you'd expect other countries to do something about it, right? Nope. It was summer, and they were all busy planning their holidays to Saint-Tropez and Ibiza. I mean, *Aibeesssaaaa*. So, as soon as he could, my father flew to Sicily. His friends tried to escape on rubber boats. So lame, right? None of his friends made it to land. All those dead bodies were like an all-you-can-eat buffet for the fishes. This was kind of great for them because the maritime fauna grew 60% in the Mediterranean Sea.

Anyway, from Sicily, my father went to Naples. He stopped there because the city reminded him of Istanbul: the music, the smell, and the hairy, loud people. He met my mother in Naples ... Carmela, the most beautiful girl he had ever seen. Her eyes were Syrian; he used to tell me. So, anyway, they got married, and then I was born. It didn't take long for my father to forget what he was running from. We were happy, a perfect Italian stereotype: my father getting mad at the television for the fixed football games, my mother arguing with the ladies at the market. Then one day, the news reported the first attacks in Syracuse.' Lucretia shivered.

'My father went crazy; he had already seen hell twice, and there was no escape from it. But long story short, the North of Italy stopped communications and cut all connections with the South. Then there was a referendum, and people decided to sell the regions north of Rome to France, Switzerland, and Slovenia, the countries that would have survived the MF. No one cared about the South, which was full of what they called white niggers anyway.

We were left to ourselves, and after one year, the situation was unbearable: food shortages, power struggles among the rebels, the mafia lords who in all this mess still expected people to kiss their hands, and MF, of course. Then, on the 21st of September, Salerno was taken. That morning, my father made us breakfast, shaved his beard, and shot himself.'

Chekhov flinched. Lucretia's dad had killed himself, just like his mother, on that same day. He started to look at her differently. All her first-world problems now collided with the reality of war. He began to think that maybe it wasn't really her fault that she was such a bitch. Perhaps it was just a shield she used to protect herself from all the tragedy around her. He thought of all those people who were not doing anything. But then again, what could they do? There was nothing to do besides wait and hope that your country would not be taken next.

'That same day, my mom and I came here. We didn't even bury my father; we just left him there and locked the door. I left windows open because he loved the smell of the sea. I like to think he's still there decomposing on the couch in front of the television, like me every weekend.'

Was there anything else to do apart from signing and sharing petitions online? Did signing help dying children in Yemen? Did liking posts on Instagram stop aeroplanes from dropping bombs? Stop men from raping women, or men from raping children, or men from raping men raping women and children? Probably not, and all these terrifying stories slowly fell into the junk inbox along with the emails from Amnesty International and Doctors Without Borders.

'Hey, you know what? You are fucking unbelievable. You deserve a prize for listening to me for so long. Don't ask questions if you are not ready to hear the answers.'

Lucretia noticed the different look in his eyes, but she kept speaking. She had no desire to indulge in sentimental exchanges of pity.

'It's just that my mother died on the same day,' Chekhovich stuttered.

'Oh, some cosmic shit going on here, right?'

'Right.'

Atomic explosions, Vesuvian eruptions, his mother's funeral. Everything played in Chekhovich's mind as he curled his lips towards Lucretia. Then, he closed one eye, leaving the other open to check her reaction, like riding a bike holding one of the brakes just in case.

As if it was nothing, Lucretia swooped in and grabbed his wrist to check the time.

'Isn't the captain waiting for us or something?'

'Yes ... that's why we're leaving ... now.' He hesitated, hoping Lucretia would linger a moment longer. 'Yes, we are going back to Marxim's farm, which is a farm and not an escort summit, so I really don't get why you packed so much latex?' he said nervously, getting up.

'Do you think the captain's gonna be happy to see me?'

'I am sure he doesn't really care, as long as he gets his carobs.'

'Yes, whatever. How do you know him anyway?'

'I wrote an article about him. He didn't like it much.'

'Too bad he didn't turn you into a pig too. I still can't believe that banquet today.'

'I can't believe we didn't touch anything!'

'We are like so vegan right now.'

They nodded at each other with approval and pride.

'Right, let's go. And don't forget your teenage prostitute kit.'

* * *

Lucretia and Chekhovich sat at Marxim's table while he carefully selected the most rotten-looking apples from a wooden box. Then, pretending not to see the occasional invertebrates roaming around the apples, Chekhovich started to speak with Lucretia.

'We haven't got much time. We need to find what this key opens, decide what do to with A'lex, think about–'

'Dinner?' Lucretia interrupted him, slamming the Belvedere on the table.

'No, the key. But, I mean, I do feel like …'

'Like a virgin?' Lucretia sang.

'What? I am not a virgin. A virgin …' he puffed like an old locomotive, 'a virgin, ahem, I am not a …'

'Touched for the very first time.' Sang Marxim, 'you sure know your music, lady, and your drinks too.' Marxim took some shot glasses. 'You are a Madonna fan?'

Lucretia nodded. 'Yes, on my mother's side.'

Marxim was now smiling at Lucretia through his Belvedere, which his rough hands held like fine china. Silenced again, Chekhovich felt so stupid for not getting the cultural reference and watched the others talk. Just like in high school. Or in university. Or the chicken shop, the barber, and the pub, and any day of his life.

Marxim nodded back. '100 looking 40.'

'Yes, I heard it's that hot yoga.'

'Yes, hot yoga. Does miracles for your body.'

Everybody nodded.

'Guys, focus!' Chekhovich shouted.

'Right, dinner. I have got some Everything Frozen in the freezer.'

'Yes? Please tell me you have the strawberry and garlic fish mash! That's my favourite.'

'Yes, I got that and the orange truffle parmesan duck.'

'The best is the coffee-bana and tuna cheese.'

'Mmm … Nutella salmon and cauliflower blue cheese.'

'Oh salmontella, yummy!'

The three started humming the jingle of the Everything Frozen, drooling. *'Na nana na na … Everything Frozen!'*

In the corner of the rustic kitchen, A'lex gagged, looking at the wasted humanity. He thought of his high-class dinners of pasta and beans served in oyster shells. Another trend he could never indulge in. Pasta and beans used to be the food for the poorest; now, it was the most expensive restaurant delicacy. There was a kind of romanticism that went along with the past. Unsatisfied in the present, people dwelled in their distorted vision of the olden days. While the poor craved the wealth of the rich, the rich longed for the virtue of the poor. And when the rich had taken everything, betrayed happiness, and fulfilled their desire, the only thing left was to take possession of the life of the poor, which wasn't a big deal because the poor, who would never be entirely satisfied, could never be unhappy. Had he still been a man, A'lex would have thought these 'high' thoughts. But he was now a pig, and he could just imagine the trash he was about to be served while aggressively munching his acorns.

A'lex looked at Lucretia, a giantess, at least from where he stood. She had never been so desirable in her almighty beauty. He used to think that she had a fat ass and hair that didn't match her chubby wrists and feet that didn't compliment the floor, but he was a pig now, and everything was better, immaculate, and pure. After those pleasant thoughts, A'lex suddenly became sad. To console him, Captain Grunter pushed a bowl of rotten apples towards him. A'lex's eyes filled with tears and disgust as he saw tiny worms crawling out of the brown spots in the apples. Then, encouragingly, the captain pushed the bowl even closer to him and amicably started a conversation in Piggish.

'It's delicious; try it.'

'No. I refuse. Change me back to human, now ... I mean, please!'

Although the aroma of the rotten fruit smelt exquisite to A'lex's nostrils, he still refused. The captain pushed A'lex's face into the bowl and raised his voice.

'You're gonna love it, trust me.'

'No, please. I am a human, we don't eat this.'

From the outside, it looked like the two pigs were fighting. The humans stopped their debates about the best Everything Frozen flavours and stared at them for a moment.

'Whatever it is, he deserves it,' Lucretia said, shrugging her shoulders.

A'lex still had his face deep in the bowl. He begged the captain to stop pushing his head. He offered money, he promised anything he had, while the juicy worm was now on top of the apple and dangerously close to his face. He started to shout about the important people he knew, people who would have looked for him and ended the world at his command, but somehow, seconds before the worm *wormed* into his nostril, A'lex mercilessly bit the apple. Crying, he kept devouring the rotten fruits until moans of pleasure replaced the whining. The captain joined the feast, and they ate until they fell asleep next to each other.

* * *

'That shit was good.' Marxim unbuttoned his pants while everyone nodded.

'So, about the key …' said Chekhovich, breaking the digestive silence.

'Yes, I got four possible addresses we should check. Two are in England, one in Holland, and the last in Guadeloupe, whoop whoop! Tomorrow, before I go to work, I'll ask A'lex which one it is.'

'What makes you think he will tell us?'

'I have my ways.' She winked.

'Are you sure you want to go to work tomorrow? I could make breakfast, like real breakfast, no Everything Frozen. Orange juice, croissants, eggs, crepes, and then we could ...'

'Thank you, but I got to go, or it will look suspicious. Plus, we are out of drinks.'

Marxim nodded forlornly. 'Well, Ceko, you guys can sleep on the futon in the guestroom.'

'Shall I sleep there as well?'

'Lucretia, you are a lady. You sleep wherever you want,' Maxim said, pointing the way. 'Goodnight, guys, and be good guys.' Marxim smiled wearily and disappeared in the darkness upstairs.

Thinking *carpe diem*, Chekhovich found the courage to finally make a move, a sexy move, or just a pathetic romantic move. His voice was shaking. 'Do you want to?'

Lucretia chugged the last shot of vodka and shook her shoulders. 'As if! Night, hun, I have a big day tomorrow.' She walked away, leaving Chekhovich alone in the kitchen.

From his rucksack, he took out his writing kit. He wanted to draft a plan of action for the day after and the days yet to come, a strategy for all the days until discovering the truth: the Great Avocado War, the Chickenocide, the Bacon Wave, everything. But he had never been a man of action, and he fell asleep in that same spot almost immediately.

* * *

Chekhovich woke up to the sight of Lucretia sitting at the table with A'lex. She was pointing at four different papers while stroking his hairy back, softly whispering into his ear to pick one of the four addresses, asking him to be a good little piglet. Chekhovich watched Lucretia's hand slowly slide down the back of the pig, smiling, biting her lips, touching her hair – all basics from the seduction manual. He kept watching while she kissed his pork rind and gently asked him, 'Come on, baby, which one?'

He saw Lucretia's fingers dangerously slide down A'lex's back. Then suddenly, A'lex screamed in ecstasy, frantically bashing his hoof on one of the pieces of paper. Lucretia removed her fingers from A'lex's body and, noticing the shock on Chekhovich's face, rolled her eyes.

'Lucretia! I can never unsee that.'

'Thanks, Lucretia, for finding what that stupid key opens. You are so indispensable, Lucretia.'

'That was so disgusting.'

'What? I used to do this even when he was human and without getting anything back.'

'But he's a pig now.'

'Aren't we all?'

A'lex stroked his head against Lucretia's breasts, pushing it between her ribs and her arm. He was begging for cuddles she was not willing to give. Finally, Lucretia told him to get lost, slapping him so violently he fell from the chair. Running outside, A'lex cried because he had feelings, and he wasn't just a toy; he was an animal. But Lucretia didn't care. She put her shoes on and started to get ready to leave for work when Marxim entered the kitchen.

'Morning, people! Breakfast anyone?' he said, remembering the best days of his life when he was just a child lost in snot and his father's hugs, who every morning would come down to cook breakfast for his family.

As if under a spell, Lucretia sat again, under Chekhovich's inquisitive look. 'I thought you were leaving.'

'I mean, it's not like my boss is gonna yell at me.'

Chekhovich shook his head at her lack of professionalism. 'Marxim, we have some developments. Lucretia found the address of the key.'

'Yeah, I did, which reminds me, I should probably wash my hands.'

'Or cut your fingers,' Chekhovich mumbled.

'What's up with you, Ceko? You in love?'

'W-we should talk about what we are going to do with the thing.' Chekhovich choked under pressure, and Marxim found it amusing.

'W-what t-thing?'

'Well, that thing. The thing, for which,' Chekhovich cleared his throat, 'we started doing … things.'

Marxim was now over Chekhovich's goofiness and started talking with Lucretia about the breakfast options.

'Eggs or cereal?'

'Ahem, what eggs have you got?'

'Lizard and …' Marxim looked in the cupboard, 'just lizard. No, also robin.'

'I like lizard eggs, but they are so freaking small. It takes a dozen to make me full.'

'It's a delicatessen. It's supposed to be this small.

When things are big, they aren't worth much.'

'Unless you are talking about d–' Lucretia nudged Ceko.

As Marxim broke the eggs into a mug, he spoke, 'I had a dream.'

Chekhovich realised how pathetic Marxim sounded since people didn't really have dreams anymore. The brain faded; ideals were overshadowed by debates about different kinds of eggs. After all, you could not touch ideals, but you could touch eggs, chairs, and things. Humans had fully evolved to be a sensorial species rather than metaphysical, which was why no one had discovered the truth yet, because they didn't care. Journalists, freedom fighters, idealists – they were romantics. They planned complex revolutions that only happened on Twitter. They bought camouflage leggings, bomb-proof mascara, and all the equipment. They spent the day watching TV, talking about the complex revolutions they would plan the day after.

Even the ordinary people didn't get anything done anymore, always stuck in their dramas: breakfast, sex, and Amazon deliveries. Everything was bound to repeat, and everything was always the same; they didn't even notice it.

'So, what are we eating?' Chekhovich had gotten lost in his thoughts.

'Eggs or cereal. Both if you want.'

'What type of eggs?' Lucretia asked again.

'Lizard or robin.'

'I love lizard eggs, but they are so tiny.' Lucretia nodded, waiting for other nodding heads to support her statement.

'They are supposed to! When things are big, they aren't much worth it. Did I tell you about the dream I had last night?'

Outside, Captain Grunter was playing football. It was his favourite game. He threw the ball at A'lex, but he missed it. He seemed worried, restlessly trotting around a small pond. The captain left the ball and moved closer to the pig apprentice.

'What's up, mate?'

'I … I need to use the bathroom.'

'The bathroom? You are a pig! Just do it here.'

'Here where?'

'Like here – here, mate.'

'But you are looking right at me.'

'It's kinkier this way. Trust me, let's do it together.'

Slowly forgetting his reluctance, A'lex dumped his load while looking straight into the captain's eyes. He was suddenly happy, probably the happiest he had been in a while.

'That was easy. It must be the high fibre dinner from last night.'

'And now do this.'

The captain jumped on the smocking pile of manure and started dancing around. A'lex wanted to question the idea, but he didn't; a new impulse told him to join the captain. So, they both jumped on the dung and rolled in it until they reached the mud around the pond. They rolled and laughed and no longer knew what was shit and what was dirt, but it didn't really matter anyway.

Exhausted, the pigs laid on the grass looking at the horizon – the house.

'So, what's the deal with you and the babe?'

'Who? Lucretia? We sort of had a thing before, but now ... we can't even talk.'

'Is that really important?'

'Of course, otherwise, how can I tell her to shut up or suck my balls?'

'Well, now you can shit wherever you want. You get to say whatever you want whenever you want. You eat and sleep, and did I mention you shit everywhere? Anytime you want, mate. And the mud fights, the baths in the pond. I'm telling you, it's just bliss. Enjoy it.'

'Let me try something.'

A'lex ran inside, oinking the equivalent of 'fuck-shit-piss-anal-cunt-balls' and rushed back outside towards the captain. He was ecstatic, choking on his own laughs.

'You're right. What's next on the piggy agenda? I wanna do it all.'

'Nothing much. We sleep, we eat, we oink. In fact, you can oink me what happened to Maria and Pepe.'

'Who?'

'The guys from your vision.'

'Oh, yea. They are dead.'

'You mean like dead to you or ...'

'Proper dead.'

'But who are they? Why did I go straight to that memory?'

'Lol, I don't ... oink.'

A'lex started to make less and less sense. His basic but elegant piggish was now mostly a confusing mess of grunts.

'Oink ... no ... I don't oink.'

'What's happening to you? Are you alright, mate?'

'Maybe I should oink down a little.'

A'lex collapsed on the ground and started to snore. Captain Grunter shrugged his shoulders and sashayed towards the house, towards his fans.

*　*　*

Chekhovich had only known Lucretia for one day, but he missed her. Thinking about her was like being punched from the inside, like listening to Bach's Cello Suite N1 in G major. But he had no words to express that. He only had his cosmic loneliness and his efforts in finding the truth that the government wanted to keep hidden. He laid his head on the table next to the plate of peas and chocolate rice he had prepared for Lucretia and fell asleep. When she got back from work, it was 3:00 a.m. Hearing the thunder of her steps, Chekhovich jumped up, dried the saliva dripping from his mouth, and rushed to the futon, pretending to be asleep. A few minutes after, Lucretia laid next to him.

'Aren't you even gonna ask me how my day was? Because you should know, Greta and Grace got back together, and I don't understand why. She's got such a nasty, nasty mouth.'

Her speech became slurred. She tied her long brown hair and started kissing Chekhovich's neck. She caressed his two-pack, but he was a strong independent man who needed no woman. Also, he did not know what to do. How long did she have to stroke Chekhovich's flaccid masculinity before she could have him? 'WHY WON'T YOU HAVE SEX WITH ME?' Lucretia yelled in an animalistic voice before falling asleep.

***

The morning after, Chekhovich was silent, Lucretia was silent, and A'lex was dead (dead asleep). Captain Grunter tried to wake him up, but he just grunted angrily, kicking him away.

Marxim was in the garden, carefully picking the smallest oranges on the tree when the captain rushed towards him.

'Marxim,' he connected telepathically to him, 'I think something is wrong with A'lex.'

'Morning, my beautiful! What's wrong with him? Troubles adjusting to the new life?'

'No, not like that. It's like … he's fading away.'

'What do you mean? You have known the pig for two days.'

'A pig just knows about pigs. A'lex is behaving like a fucking uncivilised boar. He's forgotten how to … be human, I'm telling you.'

'Maybe he is just tired. Keep talking to him, try getting something out of him.'

'What if when I extracted the memory, I fried his piggy brain? Maybe I'm the one turning him into a boar.'

Marxim placed the last orange in his bucket and patted the captain, asking him to go back to the house, reminding him he was the good guy.

Once they entered the kitchen, they saw Chekhovich and Lucretia standing silently like wax statues and A'lex on the floor. Grinning, Marxim started to cut the oranges, inebriated by their flowery scent while Chekhovich, lost in his autumnal nostalgia, sighed. He thought of all the Sundays he spent with his mother watching the 5Minutes-Hack-Guys on YouTube and never actually made anything. Then, he remembered his mother's favourite tutorial, '16 Plastic Bottles Recycle Hack.' The first time they watched it, his mother liked it so much that she immediately drove him to the nearest shop to buy 20 bottles of Coke.

'Mum, are we gonna drink all that?' little Ceko asked in awe.

'Oh, no, darling, too much sugar. But we need to buy more plastic if we want to recycle more plastic! Isn't recycling fantastic?'

Back then, that was what being a liberal meant. And people were even proud of it. Chekhovich's mother emptied the bottles in the sink and placed them in a plastic shopping bag with the Amazon jungle printed on it. Its colours, so vivid and vibrant, clashed with the view from his kitchen window. Everything was grey, a graveyard of civilisation. Chekhovich's trip to the past was interrupted by A'lex's farts, bombs that preceded fireworks of shit. Chekhovich's memories shattered, and the citrus scent transmuted in a bouquet of sewer gas and rotten meat. He looked at Lucretia, disgusted.

'And that's your ex, nice.'

'And that's your ex,' retorted Lucretia, pointing at the empty chair next to him.

'Marxim, can we have breakfast outside? I'm getting dizzy.'

As the humans left, the captain stayed back to look after A'lex. He worried about him, yet he wondered if he should get inside his head again. If A'lex's mind was truly slipping away, his team didn't have much time to collect more information before his brain went boom. They needed to know, and after all, A'lex was the enemy. Rolling in dung and mud all day long didn't exactly make them allies.

But what if going into A'lex's mind harmed him further? Did enemies have rights? Maria was innocent, and yet she didn't have rights. He needed to know about her. Maybe if he entered his mind just for a bit, it wouldn't do too much damage. He remembered what Marxim used to tell him when he was only a piglet. When he was the last piglet in the world: 'Save the life of a pig, and you'll have saved the whole slaughterhouse.'

But was he indeed saving A'lex's life? Was he helping his transition into a purer being or annihilating his existence? All these thoughts confused him. He wanted to make the right decision, but there wasn't one. The captain looked at A'lex as if he were just a pawn in the game; a good pig sacrificed because of a lousy human. History had no other chance of surviving if not by repeating itself. Before he could change his mind again, the captain bit A'lex's ear, ready to steal another memory; in this one, he was in a living room. The walls were green neon, and the furniture was entirely black except for an orange leather couch where a child sucked on ribs and watched TV. The child, a fat cherub with curly hair and blue eyes, voraciously sucked on the bones. The sight of that death covered in barbecue sauce made the captain gag and the child ecstatic. Little A'lex devoured the ribs with eyes glued to the television and turned the volume up with sudden interest.

"*Each one of us is born with limitless potential, to learn, to grow. Unfortunately, as people make poor life choices, they become their own worst enemy. So, why are poor people poor? Is that typical behaviour? And would they change if given the opportunity? To find out, watch how six of the most desperate couples of Bolivia try to survive in one of the country's poorest areas. Watch them fight for the chance to be brought to EUROPE TO WORK IN ONE OF OUR FARMS. Watch them struggle, watch them celebrate. This is their story, and it's gonna be as exciting as you'd expect it because YOU are watching it, and YOU are exciting. But let's recap because you don't need to remember anything; we remember it for you. Sit back, relax, and enjoy. Last week, we saw how Jorge and Marta got intoxicated after drinking their... let's call it self-made water, shall we? BAM! HAVOC-A-DOS! They couldn't even make the effort of remaining alive. Boohoo, Jorge, and Marta. But let's talk about the winners: Marco persuaded Tonia to pretend to be pregnant and deceive Maria into giving them her liquid supply for ... the 'baby' ... of course! Poor Maria, she lost her water supply but gained a powerful smack from Pepe! Hard life, we know, but someone's gotta do it, right? Pablo and Conchita have it even tougher; they were caught chewing coca leaves to reduce their hunger, and YOU, the real democratic power of the world, have decided that their punishment should have been no food for a week. And finally, today, for our last episode, certified sex symbol Ryan Bosslick will join us in Padilla to sip Margaritas while our contestants complete their harvest, showing the world what they have produced over the past eight weeks. It will be the international bad boy Ryan Bosslick who tells us which couple has produced the most but remember that YOU have the power. They think winning is about how much they have produced but winning is about how much they can convince you that they'll never be poor again. Because YOU are special. So, by the power vested in me by Ryan Bosslick's sculpted abs and piercing blue eyes, I declare us ready ... for ... HAVOC-A-DOS.*

The captain could not believe what he was seeing. With his hoofs, he tried to push A'lex away from the TV. But it was useless because not even the captain could change the past. So, A'lex remained there, licking his chubby fingers and dazzled by the images on TV: shots of dry valleys and decadent buildings alternated to the grins of the audience in the studio.

Three emaciated couples gathered their fruits, mostly prickly pears and pomegranates. Marco and Tonia, who had even managed to grow three egg-sized avocados, smiled confidently while the others walked behind the barn to talk. Unfortunately, the subtitles for their conversations in Spanish just read 'sibilant gibberish.' A watch in the corner timed the seconds the couples were allowed to speak Spanish. As they exceeded the three minutes, an alarm went off. The contestants bowed, apologised, and returned to the front of the farm where Marco and Tonia had just finished their plea to the public. The captain raised his ears to hear better.

'Thank you, Marco and Tonia, for a very touching story and a brilliant strategy. Now it's time for Maria and Pepe. Maria ... go.'

'I'd like to thank everyone for this great experience ... I wrote a poem if you'd like to hear it. I wrote it in Spanish and in English.'

'A poem? Aren't you just full of talents, Maria! Go on.'

The captain watched Maria read the poem in Spanish while Ryan Bosslick put his hand on his heart and solemnly closed his eyes. He did not see thousands of villagers slowly approaching the farm until she finished.

'So sweet, Maria. I didn't get a word of that, but wow. And look, so sweet, all your people came to watch you read your little poem. Now read it for those who really matter, our wonderful audiences in Europe.'

Maria, a proud brown woman with oily hair and hollow cheeks, bowed at the presenter, who looked at her in a mixture of pity and lust. She was the kind of skinny that would have dominated the French catwalks and fashion shows if born on the other side of the world. She licked her dry lips.

'Stop all the farmers, turn off the ploughs. Stop shovelling shit between the furrows, and with an aching hand, dry the sweat from your forehead. Raise all the hoes. Scream from sunset to dawn of the hunger that cripples you into bed and that you can't bear the sight of your children living another day. An empty plate in front of them as they say, "Mami, don't cry; I am not hungry anyway." Gather your friends, your tools, and your thoughts. The sky will be red...'

The captain watched Ryan Bosslick going from extremely fabulous to banally worried. He gestured to the cameramen to stop filming, but they didn't. Instead, they ran away, leaving their equipment behind. From laying on the ground, the expensive camera captured hundreds of feet and Spanish chants. The studio cut the transmission. The live audience was speechless, and little A'lex punched the couch, screaming: 'Who won? I want to know who won!'

As the child writhed in anger, the captain noticed that the neon walls started melting around him, disappearing into black nothingness. Little A'lex began to turn into a pig while the captain watched the television, hoping he could find out more. Then it hit him; he had to leave A'lex's mind immediately. The television became oblivion, the bright orange couch vanished, and the light bulb dimmed to nothingness.

The captain closed his eyes, counted to ten, and then opened his eyes again. Everything was still black. Blindly, he trotted, ran, and grunted for help. No one heard him. He was now the prisoner of his victim.

* * *

Outside, Lucretia and Chekhovich sunbathed in the January sun, drinking orange juice silently. Then, noticing that it was 1:00 p.m. and Lucretia had not barked against Chekhovich yet, Marxim decided to restore the natural order of things with the century's greatest solution: small talk. Not even looking at her, he started his series of lukewarm futilities while Chekhovich looked down, mesmerised by the ginger hair on his legs.

'It's a wonderful day, isn't it, Lulu?' Marxim asked Lucretia.

'Yeah.'

'Feels almost like February, right, Ceko?'

'Yup.'

Noticing Chekhovich's calm indifference to her, Lucretia thought of a better strategy to upset him. What was the point of silence when she could hurt him with her exciting discoveries? So, she spoke with the high pitch of her best moments.

'OMG, Marxim, I forgot to tell you, yesterday I went out with the babes from work, and it was totally a blast, but then the schedule organiser bitch got really kinky with this boy and said she was gonna go home with him and didn't even invite me, so I was like fuck this shit, and I took my purse and went to the address A'lex gave me.' She finally got everyone's attention. 'Yeah, it was one of those 24h banks, you know, one of those shitty places where they have deposit boxes. And you can like go there at night and get your wife's jewellery from the deposit box because Manson knows your escort could really use some fancy decoration—'

Chekhovich jumped up, shouting hysterically, 'Why didn't you tell me earlier? What did you find?'

'Captain, wake up. Captain!'

Marxim's excruciating scream filled the house. He was pacing around the room while gesturing in random acts of hope mixed with rage, shaking the once pinkest of pigs.

But neither his slaps nor his bites woke him.

The scene was even more confusing in Chekhovich's weepy eyes. Everything was blurred, and his friends were only spots covered by muffled sounds. Then, drying his eyes, he saw the two lifeless pigs on the kitchen floor. What happened? How could that have happened? Why did it happen?

And most importantly, did it really happen? Could it have been an illusion created by the Anticapitanists? Maybe they wanted him to go mad because they knew he was the one. They knew Chekhov Chekhovich was the chosen one and the only person who could have ever exposed the truest of the truths. They knew it, and they wanted to shut him up.

Like when as a child, he tried convincing his father not to put batteries in the trash. He tried to make him understand the dangers easily prevented just by recycling batteries the right way by throwing them in the battery bin every supermarket had, even the big Sainsbury's they always shopped from every Saturday. His father's sardonic smile as he turned up the volume of the Ted Talk he watched deafened him. Often, the sound of the informed speakers' voices had soothed his fire for justice, but on one particular day, a sparkle connected his ears to his brain. Watching the video of a man teaching the world about "how to stop watching useless videos" inspired him. Chekhovich clenched his fist, charged with rage and his little hero complex, as he walked to the bin. He saved a couple of AAs from the trash and put them in a jar of water. That would have taught his father to recycle. The world needed bold actions and audacious warriors if it wanted to survive. Again, Chekhovich stopped questioning what was in front of him. He stomped on the ground in front of the pigs as if he were in a trance. Maybe those two pigs lying on the floor were just an illusion.

'Move, you fucking zombie,' screamed Lucretia, pushing Chekhovich away. 'What happened?' she said, bending towards the swine.

The shove brought Chekhovich back to reality, and he realised he hadn't taken his happy pills since it all began, and he rose from the mediocrity of his life to accomplish the unthinkable.

Something so amazing it could have possibly even been showcased in the Museum of Twitter and Other Good Things one day.

'They have been like this for the past two days. Where the fuck were you? I tried calling you so many times,' Marxim uttered, weeping furiously.

'We went to that 24h bank,' Chekhovich pleaded but was soon interrupted.

'Don't get me wrong; I am grateful you did that one thing you offered to do and said you would do, and it only took you two days. You are a real go-getter, sport! It's just that in the meantime, I was here waiting for Godot, watching the captain rotting away.'

'Why is nobody talking about A'lex?' Lucretia asked as she grabbed the controller of an old TV and started zapping through the channels.

'That's great, isn't it?' Chekhovich asked, positively surprised that at least something wasn't going as bad as the rest.

'Are you crazy? It has been like four days now.' Lucretia counted on her fingers. 'I think. Someone must have realised A'lex is missing.'

Marxim dried his tears. 'They must know something is wrong. They must be preparing to attack. They know we went to see A'lex. You! You told them. Isn't that true, Lucretia? You sold us out, right?' Marxim raised his voice and shook Captain Grunter, whom he held in his ginger-haired arms.

'What are you talking about?' Chekhovich intervened with eyes full of terror, fearing the depth of his own doubt creeping in as Marxim accused Lucretia. He descended into the political paranoia that only a few moments ago tangoed in his head.

'You are defending your bitch girlfriend now? Eh, Bigballscevich?'

Annoyed more than offended, Lucretia replied to Marxim. She dragged a wooden chair closer to him and sat down. She spread her legs and bent down, almost like a giraffe drinking from a water hole. 'Look, I know you are in pain and that you don't even really know me but before you start breaking my balls with your *J'accuse*, hear me out. Look at the facts: one, I'd never sell you out. You made me breakfast, and you made it without any expired shit or discounted brands. Do you think that went unnoticed? No, it did not. I didn't sell you out. I like you guys, and I really like the captain. And as a matter of fact, I think he might really like me too, so why would I ruin this beautiful thing we might have?' Lucretia's dreamy eyes devoured the captain's corpse. 'I didn't sell you out. My family taught me manners and how to always stay on the winning side; OK, sure, it doesn't look like you are winning right now but think positive. She started counting on her fingers: 1) Good things come to those who wait; 2) Your dreams can come true if you dare to pursue them; 3) Great things never come from staying in your comfort zone; 4) Don't hate Monday, hate yourself; 5) Positive mind, positive heart, see what I mean? I didn't sell you out.'

Chekhovich shook his head at the nonsense, 'Well, to be honest, she was with me the whole time. I would have seen her doing something sketchy.'

'Oh yeah, you think so?' Lucretia smirked. 'I could take a shit in front of you, and you wouldn't notice. But yes, I was with him the whole time,' she said, caressing Marxim's head while he wept – ashamed and hopeless. 'Believe me, Marxim, everything is gonna be fine.' Lucretia gently took his face in her hands, whispering, 'But you ever call me a bitch again …

yeah?' Lucretia said, and her eyes went straight from Hannah to Tony Montana.

'Did something happen before they went in catalepsy?' Asked Chekhovich.

'When I have my period, I can sleep for months,' Lucretia answered swiftly, getting up from the chair, which she delicately pushed under the table.

Chekhovich remembered Lucretia's huge period pants and smiled.

'Perv.' Lucretia's eyes judged the bulge in Chekhovich's pants.

She hadn't noticed before, but there was always a bulge in his pants. And it would have always been. It was the last trend between men of all ages, from 10 to 100 years old. They all enhanced themselves. It was common knowledge. A filled-looking pair of pants would go a long way in finance, politics, physics, gastronomy – anywhere at all.

Between Lucretia's disgusted looks and Chekhovich's red cheeks, Marxim's whining reverberated in the room and made everyone's hair stand on end. Then, shaking the shivers off their shoulders, the lovers finally ended their quarrel.

'It's my fault,' Marxim repeated, hitting his head with strong and callous hands. 'The captain told me there was something wrong with A'lex, but I thought: OK, he's a pig now, of course, that's what's wrong with him! Stupid, stupid Marxim.' Then, again, he hit his head furiously. 'What if he got what A'lex had?'

'What A'lex had?' Lucretia was puzzled. Last time she saw A'lex, he was a happy-go-lucky piggy.

'I don't know, like something to do with the brain. I think he went back into A'lex's head.'

'But why would he? The last time was brutal. He knew he needed to recover before another. Is this pig really so insane?' Chekhovich spoke with his self-righteous attitude.

'I ... I told him to,' Marxim said, bursting into tears, 'I thought he would have been fine; I thought nothing could have hurt him apart from barbecue sauce. But I'm such a stupid shit, and now he's never coming back, fucking fuck, shit idiot.'

Marxim kept swearing, slapping his face, now flaming from the continuous hits.

'What do you mean, something wrong with A'lex?' they asked.

'I don't know. He worried about A'lex going uber-pig or something, and now they are both dead.'

'What are you talking about? They are both breathing,' Lucretia pointed out, looking at the steam in the animals' nostrils left on the pavement.

'You think so?' Marxim's eyes sparkled with hope, mucus running down his nose, which he smeared across his face trying to dry his tears.

'And how did you not see that?' Lucretia said, pointing at the huge pile of shit just behind him.

'Yeah, that looks pretty fresh to me,' added Ceko.

'Oh my, Manson! I thought ... I did that! The last few days are a bit of a blur. What? I have been pretty upset.'

Lucretia and Chekhovich's disgusted expressions found each other and climaxed in a gag.

'What if A'lex's brain collapsed while the captain was inside his mind?' Chekhovich said, talking directly at the pile. He could not take his eyes off that majestic monument to life.

'I think I might know something that could wake them up. I mean, I haven't done it for medical reasons for quite some time, but we could try.' Lucretia pulled up her sleeves and leaned towards the captain. 'I learnt this in nursing school. Trust me, this is going to fix everything. Maybe.' She knelt and looked at the pig, checked his heartbeat, inspected his ears, and lifted his right hoof just to see it drooping down limp. Marxim was still holding the pig in his big, tear-soaked arms.

Lucretia lifted her arm and closed her fingers into a fist that raced towards the anus of the hero. Then, millimetres away from the orifice, she lifted her accusing finger. Marxim promptly pushed her away, and she almost fell on the manure.

'What in the love of Manson do you think you are doing?' Marxim asked, outraged.

'What are you pushing me away for? I know how to get a pig's attention. Trust me,' she said, getting back in fingering position.

'You listen to me; you finger-blasting-b … beast!' Marxim said, grabbing her hand. 'You won't lay a finger on the captain. Do you hear me? Not on or in.'

'What if this is the only way to bring the captain back?' Chekhovich asked, not really worried about his friend's ass.

'What makes you think that? What has this story turned into? Back in my time…' Marxim tried using the past to shield the captain's bum, but the past, just like the present and surely the future, was indeed a continuous cycle of butt-fucking.

'There's only a 40% chance of becoming a homophile if that's what you are worried about,' Lucretia said, checking the statistics on FB like a professional and informed secretary.

'A finger in the bum doesn't actually make you gay, does it?' Chekhovich asked, concerned.

'Why would I care about that? I have seen more dicks than you have seen stars, you stupid twerp.'

'Then what's the problem?' Lucretia asked.

'I … I don't want his first time to be like that.'

'Oh, my Manson, would you like to do the honours?' Lucretia asked, backing away from the anus.

'Fuck no,' Marxim said, abhorred.

'No, really, we can leave you two alone if you'd like.

Maybe get some lavender candles, coconut condoms …'

'Shut up!' Marxim exploded. 'What if it's like Samson's hair? What if he loses his powers?'

'Marxim look, we have all seen the shits the pig takes; there is no way that asshole is still intact,' Chekhovich said, patting Marxim on the back.

'Look, it's a real thing,' said Lucretia, turning on her mind searcher. 'Europe's health system has already added APR to CPR.'

The images of finger positions and anal cavities shone on the wet irises of Marxim's eyes.

'APR?' asked Marxim, curious and estranged.

'Anal Probing Resurrection.'

'Oh no, see, the R stands for reanimation,' Chekhovich corrected her.

'Well, yes, initially. But as 97% of the patients got an erection during or after the procedure, they decided to change reanimation with resurrection. See, everything is written here,'

Lucretia said, pointing at a 2022 research from Cambridge University.

'Well, that does make sense.' Marxim nodded.

'Where do you even get your news?' Chekhovich asked, annoyed.

'Babes, I don't get news. I make news.'

'Just stop fighting. Fine, let's do it. We can't waste any more time but listen to me and listen carefully. If someone's gonna blast my piggy, it's gonna be me. I'm family, after all.'

'If you can't trust your family to finger you in your moment of need, then who can you trust?' Lucretia solemnly nodded.

'Plus … we got nothing to lose, right?' Chekhovich added, looking at Lucretia, who had disgust printed in each grimace of her face.

'First, tell me what you found in the bank. There might be something helpful.'

'I'll get you some coffee.'

While Lucretia was in the kitchen preparing the potion, Chekhovich pulled Marxim up and helped him sit on a chair. As he got up, an earthy stench filled the room.

'So, what did you find? Why did you take so long to come back?' In Marxim's eyes, anger had been replaced by affliction.

Chekhovich hesitated, squinted, and moved his face to the other side. Not because he felt guilty or somehow responsible about what happened but because he didn't want to open his mouth so close to Marxim's stench. They sat one in front of another. Then, pulling and tormenting his cuticles, Chekhovich started his tale.

'Well, let me start by reminding you that we left on a Friday, and as you know, because on the weekend most factories are not working, we couldn't just walk around the streets without, like, high enough levels of carbon dioxide in the air. You know three people died last month because of that, remember? One of them was like the leader for the free hate speech movement, and honestly, I have always had breathing problems like even when I ...' Marxim stared at Chekhovich empty-eyed as if hundreds of years had passed since he started talking.

'So, first, we went to eat. Lots of eggs. Then we had to wait to digest and wait for the sulphur emission machine.'

'Sulphur emission ... what are you talking about?' asked Marxim, confused and irritated.

'I mean our butts.'

'It took you two days out of the mission to fart on each other? Is that some niche mating ritual?'

'Don't you listen to me? We cannot breathe clean oxygen. We'll die, I don't know if you haven't noticed, but we have evolved; we cannot breathe pure oxygen without dying.'

Marxim huffed away in disbelief. Back in his time, farting used to mean something. It used to be something special, something that could be cherished in solitude or shared with an oblivious audience. There were mostly two schools of thought. Some people waited for the train to reach the platform before unloading their belly – so everyone could smell. Still, no one could judge, as both the roar and the smell were completely covered and overcome by the noise and the stench that the train brought with itself from the bowels of the city. That was what good citizens did. Another approach was contemplating farting as the communal activity par excellence; people were dropping one while queuing for the check-in on their flights, in classes, shops, anywhere a fart could be smelt but not seen. This was mostly the way of the psychopaths and adventure seekers. The tang filling the nostrils of oblivious strangers was the real kick for them more than the liberation from the gas. Nobody would have ever done anything about it, no one could even know with certainty who the culprit was, and that gave the offender a sense of omnipotence. No restraints, no guilt, no consequences, just farts.

Apart from that, back in Marxim's time, farting also had a sentimental value. It was proof of the union of a couple. The immense sacrifice of binding your buttocks in front of the other on a seemingly endless first date was the primary indicator that the relationship was worth pursuing. Enduring a night of stomach cramps was the ultimate declaration of love. Back in his time, farting was a little secret to be caged and released, at least until the first "I love you." Now? People farted because they had to, not because they wanted to. What a sad life that was. Romance was dead, and freedom was ancient history.

'So, after we got our fart protection shield, the first thing we found was that the 24h bank was actually just a 2-4h bank. Needless to say, we went there just after closing. So, we went back to the restaurant, ate more eggs, and waited some more.'

'Why didn't you come back here? Why would you spend two days in a restaurant? Ceko, don't lie to me.'

'That is the truth. We ate the eggs. We waited for the farts, and without the captain checking the contamination levels in the air, the farting was essential, you know? So, I thought since we were already out, we might just find a little place over the letame.'

'Letame?'

'Le Thames ... sorry, I speak French when I get ... ahem ... anyway, every time we tried going to the bank, it was always closed, so we ended up going back to Lucretia's just to feed Tom.'

'What the fuck are you saying? Ceko, you make no sense. "Feed Tom." Is that a euphemism? You were fucking, eh? So, you are telling me the reason you weren't here while the captain and I needed you was because you wanted to get some?'

Chekhovich's face was incandescent like lava, while Marxim's inquisitionist-like tone turned into a more impressed one.

'No, it's nothing like that. I didn't fuck her!'

Chekhovich screamed, violently punching the table.

'So, what did you do during those two days?'

Chekhovich crumbled under all the pressure and the prestige that came with being a fuck boy. He cried.

'The truth is that after we went to the restaurant the first time, we kinda forgot what we went out to do, and we went back to Lucretia's place. She said she wanted to feed the dog or feel the dog, one of the two. I didn't hear it, all right? So, I thought, OK, let's see what she was talking about, and then, when we arrived, she had to pee. I turned on the TV for five minutes, and ...'

'And then we watched some internet.' Lucretia interjected as she came back with the mugs. Her eyes glued to the chocolate oak laminated parquet. 'We sat down and never got up except for bathroom breaks and food pick-ups,' she said, slamming the mugs on the table, ashamed and repentant.

Then Chekhovich took the stand, vigorously getting up from his chair and walking off, pleading his case to a sparkling clean stone fireplace. 'The truth is that we fell asleep and could never wake up on time. Do you know, Marxim, how hard it is?' he said, turning towards him in a crescendo. 'Do you know how hard it is to fall asleep at 3 a.m. and get up at 7?'

'On a weekend!' shouted Lucretia, lowering her guilt-ridden face.

'Yes, maybe we should have never even tried taking the situation into our own hands. We should have had you going to that bank. Maybe if you were with us, things would have been different,' Chekhovich said, nervously walking back and forward to the stone fireplace. Resentment burned like a UTI, and he bashed his fist to the wall multiple times until Lucretia, full of sorrow, stopped his hand.

'The truth is that we just can't wake up on time, and without our soya-mocha-no-foam-lattes, we are basically useless; we know it, you know it. But isn't this how you raised us to be? Isn't this how you want us to be?'

In Lucretia's hands, Chekhovich again found the strength to vouch for his truth. 'Yes, so you can keep going with that 'back in my time' bullshit and feel so mighty and omnipotent. But I'm telling you that if there were any internet back in any Manson-damned age in history, nobody would have gotten anything done anyway!'

Marxim was shocked and disappointed in his partners, but again, not surprised.

'You are pathetic,' Marxim said, getting up from the chair and brushing off a dry brown chip stuck to his arm. 'How old are you? Behave like grown-ups for once in your life. Haven't you already watched all of the internet?' He couldn't believe there was still someone who hadn't watched it all. He was 70 years old, and he had seen it all twice.

Lucretia and Chekhovich exchanged sympathetic looks. How could Marxim be so naïve? Then, the two moved back from the fireplace and walked towards him, cautiously trying not to break Marxim's delicate state of mind.

'But Marxim,' Lucretia said, putting her hand on this big and sweaty shoulder, 'the internet is always rebuilding itself. How could we ever watch it all?'

Chekhovich accompanied Marxim back to his seat. He didn't believe them; they were young and lazy and therefore capable of making up anything to escape his furious-but-fair judgement.

'Yeah, think about it. Once you have seen all the videos in the world, new ones come up. Videos of people watching videos, then videos of people commenting on people watching videos; it's a never-ending vortex.'

Marxim felt something scratching in his throat. He grabbed a sip of coffee and tried to get up, his reality was crumbling, and he wanted to hold the captain. As he got up, he felt like he was descending down a vortex. He collapsed onto the chair again, grasping the edge of the chipped chestnut table tightly.

The advent of the internet marked a time when the audience was no longer subject to the tyrannical broadcast era, with its little choice of programming and long commercial breaks. At the same time, as people became so undeniably immersed in a visual culture made by constructions and deconstructions of the world, people could see everything without going anywhere, and that created a kind of hysteria in the audience; a feeling of omnipotence coming from the 'all you can eat' entertainment. This turned the once active audience into a subject again. In this context, entertainment became a kind of war by proxy, fought on the screens of millions of devices that could comfortably be played-paused-replayed and won through views and ratings. Much tidier than traditional wars and perfect for lazy millennials.

'The internet is like the labour market, always reinventing itself, shifting its needs and always erasing and creating new jobs,' Chekhovich informed.

'Yeah, remember when they cancelled all the nail whisperers, and all of them got converted into ball-jewellery makers?' Lucretia shook her hands to the sky. She still could not get over the shocking news.

Marxim felt stupid, hopelessly thinking about how much he missed and wasn't even aware of. Defeated, he got up and left the table to the people of culture and once again sat on the floor, completely alienated, caressing the comatose pigs. The smell didn't bother him; it rather inspired him. It was the kind of stench that opens your lungs and makes you want to die. But, after all, aren't those the moments when we feel most alive?

'What was that other thing with the PCP?' Lucretia took a sip of the coffee that was now lukewarm and disgusting. 'I never actually got that. Are the PCP the people who take your leftovers at restaurants?'

'Well, kinda,' Marxim spoke, still cuddling the pigs, cheered up by the fact he still knew something. 'That was the original meaning, but the PCP is mostly used to address those guys in grey shirts. You know, the ones holding baskets for the refuse. Like bins but more interactive – always saying good morning, thank you, bye and all that, and they only do plastics anyway, so it's a bit niche.'

'Well, is there anything out there that isn't made of plastic?' Lucretia asked.

'The PCP policy was such a revolutionary initiative. It gave back so many jobs to those who became obsolete with the industrial progress. It gave people back a way to feed their family, gave them dignity,' Chekhovich said, righteous and proud of his communist propaganda.

'Dignity, you say? Think of all those chemical engineers turning PCP ... standing, living garbage bins. Sorry, plastic bins,' Lucretia said with a finger quote to every word she uttered. Again, they started bickering. In the meantime, Marxim was back in his trance, nodding and lulling the captain, staring at the full-bodied grey sky he saw between each small rectangle of the black metal grating that defended his reign from the ill-intentioned. The truth was that nobody ever came around his farm. Crime had been defeated a long time ago, somewhere between the first wave of deaths from CO_2 and O, and The Great Avocado War. The few lucky survivors of these catastrophes didn't need to steal from each other anymore; their government did it for them. Why would anyone even get up from their comfy bed to rob a shabby farm in Essex when they had their government robbing entire nations? It was not only unneeded but very belittling. Marxim kept staring at the sky until he heard the first of three thunder strikes that, like a stomach cramp after dairy, warned him about an impending menace. A tempest of hot rain gushed from the sky, and he woke up. 'Are you ever gonna tell me what happened in these two days? What did you find at the bank?'

'Yes, I am sorry, Marxim. After a couple of days of vegetating, Ceko and I finally realised it was time to go – meaning we had no food and were hungry. So, on Monday, we went to the bank, first thing in the morning after breakfast. We got in Ceko's pathetic car, and the last movement of the Piano Concerto No.13 in C major was playing. The worst, right?'

'Mozart?' Marxim asked. He knew that Monday to Friday radios were only playing Mozart, but it was always nice joining in a conversation with the certainty of having the correct answer.

'What else? It was a Monday! Anyway, why the worst, you'd ask, well …' Lucretia said in her best teacher impression, 'I find the minor key section to be highly awkward.'

'For two reasons!' anticipated Chekhovich with confidence, as he had already had this same conversation with her.

'First,' Lucretia continued, 'it comes too early in the piece.'

Chekhovich silently repeated each and every word Lucretia spoke. 'And second, in my opinion, it sounds quite contrived. Kitsch, if you may …'

'Yes! Because it is repeated,' Chekhovich said, losing his patience. 'A dramatic interpolation loses its power once repeated.'

Marxim paused and nodded. 'Yeah, it definitely does when you think about it.'

Lucretia continued, 'The first movement is not as bad, but still quite bad.'

All nodded for endless seconds until Marxim intervened, 'So, you are driving the shit mobile, and the radio is playing shit. What then?'

'Yes, we said we were going to the bank, so we did. When we entered, it was just as you would expect a 2-4h bank to be— dark walls and neon lighting, rivers of white matter all over the walls. On the first floor, these two hunks were checking their deposits. Initially, I felt bad for them for having their deposits on the ground floor, like who does that? Then I thought they were young and dumb, probably full of cum. They might want to get in and get out as soon as possible, go back to the babes waiting in the car. So, I looked, I objectified, moved to the second floor making sure they were looking at my ass, and when I was really sure they were looking, I turned towards them with the meanest look, 'What are you looking at, perverts?'

Lucretia took small pauses after each sentence just to observe the two guys and ensure they were listening. 'We kept walking through the floors trying to avoid the dirty underwear and receipts scattered on the ground until we got to the 4th, N 425-AA. We arrived at the deposit box, cold, grey, and dead. I almost opened it. YOLO, you know? But then I think: nobody in their right mind would leave their babes in the car. Babes don't wait in the car. With real babes, you snooze, you lose.'

'What are you talking about?' Marxim inquired, looking at Chekhovich, who seemed doubtful himself.

'No, the motto is, you jizz you leave,' Chekhovich corrected her.

'No, it's like, jizz is biz. Or something.'

Marxim was even more confused now and prayed for them to get to the point.

'Come on, Marxim, you know what we are talking about. Babes? The entrepreneurs, you caveman! Remember that wave of YouTubers in 2015 that became millionaires making videos of swallowing condoms or sucking used tampons? Babes are kinda the same but with brains. Who knew that working in customer service could actually work out! They have that *je ne sais quoi*. Plus, they are great for the economy. Their business brings a 13% annual revenue increase to the state, and that's for hand stuff only. Impressive, right?'

'I thought the "babes" had been banned,' Marxim said.

'Banned? Never! They can't close our legs, but they can put a tax on it. Sad, but it makes sense, don't you think? I'd do it too if I didn't have haemorrhoids.'

'What's a couple of haemorrhoids matter in the grand scheme of things? I really didn't think the babes business had such rigorous requirements.'

'No, it's actually a pretty accepting environment. In my case, it's more of a judgement call. I mean, who would want to fuck with someone bleeding out their ass half of the time?'

'Yeah, nobody would,' Chekhovich answered, disgusted but excited to learn new things about Lucretia.

'I mean, I am sure I would be pigeonholed to a niche, and pretty soon, I'd mostly receive requests from perverts.'

'And sadists,' he continued.

'No, no sadist would pay for something bleeding before they put their hands on it. Where's the satisfaction in that?' Lucretia said, gesticulating like a mad genius. 'Just think.'

A long moment of silence followed, and everybody avoided looking at her.

Another thunderclap roared in the sky.

'Guys!' Marxim was still aching for the rest of the story. He couldn't feel his hands anymore, but he kept caressing the captain's rough back.

'Sorry. So, we were going back down, and those two guys were still there.'

'I thought they might be spies,' Lucretia interrupted, 'so I decided not to open the box in the bank.'

'Instead, she decided to go straight to them and slut around,' Chekhovich said, pointing out and ridiculing her behaviour.

'I decided to engage them, catch them by surprise. If we had anything to hide, we would have acted weird – tried to avoid any kind of contact, right?'

'Right, so she goes to those guys and makes a 'babe' out of herself.'

'They were both Swedish. The Swedish make good spies, I thought. Tall, blond braids like Vikings, and shoulders wide like Ikea PAX closets. Blue eyes, milky skin, bla bla, you get the idea. I think they were twins.'

'Well, you think all blond people look alike.'

'So, they were whitewashed versions of Ceko?' Marxim asked.

'They were nothing like Ceko. Don't say that ever again. They were all like "mhmm," and Ceko is all like "uhgh-uh,"' Lucretia said, shrugging her shoulders. 'Anyway, after the usual, "what's your name? How much you earn?" they asked me if I wanted to go to their place.'

'They actually wanted me to go,' Chekhovich said.

'Guys always hit on the less attractive friend first; you know that.'

'They said that you could have come along only if I had gone!'

'Obviously, they were just playing hard to get.'

'Yes, you were also playing hard to get. A hint!'

Lucretia saw a slight curve on Marxim's mouth. In another situation, he would have burst out laughing. Outraged, she ran around the table to stop Chekhovich from bubbling further lies, but he ran faster and kept mocking her in an anime girl voice, *'I will only come if you promise you won't touch my ass.'* And then he went back to his man voice, 'Oh, I will definitely not touch your ass.'

The damage was done. Lucretia stopped running.

'You should have seen her face,' Chekhovich said, catching a breath. 'Her eyes sparkled with pride, her cheeks blushed, and she barely kept it together. She thought the guy was super respectful.'

'Well, he gave me those "might murder you, might fall in love with you" eyes. Who doesn't like that?'

'They are Swedish, and they only have that one dead stare look! Anyway, we went with them in their car because Lucretia didn't want them to see her riding in my–'

'Turdmotor.'

'Why did you guys go with them anyway? You had the safe with you. This makes no sense,' Marxim said.

'Yeah, but just in case they really were spies, we didn't want them to follow us here.'

'Meaning she wanted to get some with one of the Hans. They lived in this huge building on top of an ex-something factory and …'

Lucretia turned on her mind recorder, and the images flashed over Marxim's eyes. Sanguine bricks were carefully layered on top of each. Others extended vertically for five floors. In line with the third floor, a metal signboard elongated through the whole breadth of the construction, covering part of the windows. The sign read:

EVERYTHING FACTORY

HEAD OFFICE/CAREER AND DEVELOPMENT CENTRE THINK SMALL JUST DO IT OBEY YOUR THIRST YOU'RE WORTH IT. EVERYTHING IS FOREVER.

Private Unlimited Company

'They owned the whole building, it smelled like money." Lucretia interrupted.

'Well, more like mould, really. The entrance was empty and dusty. It didn't look like anyone had been there for years.'

Spider webs followed one another on the walls and the corners of the entrance. The ceiling, black and sooty, remembered an old explosion in the main hall many years before. And on the right, faded but still legible: RICHES GET STITCHES.

'OK, you are telling it wrong. First, it was an ex-Everything Factory, and second, of course, they kept it as it is. It's a historical building. Sure, it looks like shit and smells like shit, but clean that, and you lose all the value. Anyway, Marxim, as soon as we got to the second floor ...'

They had to climb the emergency stairs to get to the second floor, where the chipped red and yellow phosphorescent paint was the only visible thing in the narrow and caliginous path. Once they reached the mezzanine, a wall lamp highlighted a door where a "BEWARE TOXIC WASTE" logo stood untarnished by time and toxicity. On the other side of the door, an ecstasy of cream coloured furniture played before their eyes. Light radiated from the windows, reflected on the worn-down honey parquet floor, and bounced onto the ivory walls. Everything was impeccable in the industrial-style living room. The room was mostly empty apart from a sand block sofa in the back of the room and a wooden-crate coffee table, which offered a place to relax and the chance to show guests the effortless coolness of the Hans. Yet, the worn and torn atmosphere clashed with the enormous diamond windows.

'So, what happened there?' Marxim asked.

'We started with drinks. After that, I minded my business, just walking around, snooping through windows, looking for a bathroom.'

Lucretia followed a large piping extractor that the floor revealed under a runway of glass. The pipes abruptly ended in front of a window from which Lucretia could see the insides of the factory's first floor. Machinery to smash, roll and cut stuff, rusty clogs abandoned on the floor and black bin bags never thrown out. For a moment, she tried to imagine the hellish noise all those machines had made in the past. It would have been hard for the workers to talk to each other during the shift, how silent it must have felt to scream between that punch press and the tumbling barrels.

Lucretia sighed. 'Then, I hear Chekhovich courting one of the Hans. Pathetic. "Bro, what do you think of the tax situation in Liberia?" Like, what the fuck does that even mean?'

'It was nothing like that, thank you. We were talking about–'

'Oh no, you are right, now I remember,' she said, breathing in and flexing her biceps, miming cavemen flirting. "Bro, you like Everything Frozen? Nutella Salmon, yeah? Yeah, bro, but it's full of sugar. Bro, but everything is fine with moderation. Yeah, bro, moderation is the name of the game"'

'Shut up; it's not my fault that you tried and failed to get the other Hans.' Again, Chekhovich did the sexy bunny voice. 'Oh,

you are the strongest Hans I have ever seen. Pants down …
I mean hands down, hi hi hi!' Chekhovich mocked Lucretia
giggling and squirming. He graciously lifted his left leg as if
he was ready to grant his first kiss to the most wonderful oil
tycoon.

'Guys, I swear to Manson, if you don't stop wasting my fucking
time,' Marxim said, his eyes blood red.

'Okay, okay, relax. To cut it short, neither of the guys actually
touched my ass, and one of them even hooked up with Ceko;
like what the fuck? Not your type, I get it, but don't waste my
time. So, at some point I got bored and opened the box. When
I saw this, I grabbed Ceko and–'

'This was inside …' Chekhovich interrupted Lucretia before
she could go on with one of her monologues. He handed over
an old photograph, which Marxim grabbed with greed as if it
belonged to him. A woman was holding hands with a perfect,
chubby child in a sailor outfit. Marxim dropped the picture
on the floor. Unfortunately, that was not something that could
have helped the captain. Chekhovich pulled something else
from his pocket full of lint and chocolate wraps. 'And this,' he
said, showing a key with a treble clef key ring. 'And … this!'
he added. 'Looks like the page of an old diary or something.'

'Well, read it!'

December 30, 2027.

I know the truth.

THE TRUEST OF THE TRUTHS

- **2017:** Russia cuts off gas as snowstorms hit Europe. Citizens freeze to **death**. Our dearest President Manson comes up with a solution: investing in the meat industry. Of course, this would mean trusting vegans and their blog posts about how the emissions from the meat plants lead to a temperature rise, but it's worth a shot. The slaughter of the animals seems to follow **the Chinese zodiac**. 2017 is the year of the Rooster. The **Chickenocide** lasts for two years.

- **2019:** Year of the Pig. The government promotes **The Bacon Wave** through a series of well-calculated Twitter storms and a mediatic avalanche of Tastyy videos showing the happiest ending for a pig: bacon chains, bacon party decorations, #BeconMyValentine for the romantics. As predicted, the sulphur and carbon dioxide emissions from the meat plants successfully lead to a **global temperature rise.**

- **2023:** No more winters. Meteorologists register storms of **hot rain** around the planet. The levels of oxygen plummet. Many die; those who survive learn how to get used to breathing carbon dioxide. On the downside, the rising **sea level** threatens to wipe off the coasts of England. Our dearest President Manson decides to solve the problem by **draining** the sea and filtering ocean water for irrigation. He buys avocado plantations in South America, financing a farmer Stakhanovite movement. The more they produce, the more first-world goods they receive: Nike hair bands, Marc Jacobs credit card holders, Chanel nail polish, and even a luminous hoverboard for whoever can collect 1000 avocados in 24 hours. Some die of fatigue, others from severe injuries after trying to protect their baskets from over-excited Stakhanovites.

- **Avocados** are now in great demand, possibly because of an extensive marketing campaign and undoubtedly because of the chemical stimulants added to the fruits, making them as addictive as crack cocaine.

- **2025:** The flourishing avocado business becomes unsustainable; the demand is so high that farmers now use drinking water for their plantations. Despite their efforts, the production cannot keep up with the demand. A progressive shortage of avocados and the delays in the deliveries to the U.K. generate the so-called **'avocado tourism.'** Sellers, businessmen, and even entire families start their peregrinations to South America to ensure they get their share of avocados.

- **2026:** The reserves **of avocados progressively diminish, leading to the Great Avocado War,** a series of violent clashes between over-excited avocado tourists and plantation workers. Tired of their inhumane living conditions and the Stakhanovism imposed upon them, farmers organise a series of guerrilla operations against the tourists. Millions die. The U.K. decrees 50 years of silence in respect for the **victims of the conflict.** Journalists and conspiracy theorists who try to investigate the matter are imprisoned and charged with Mansonism (**subversion and treason**). If you are reading, my dears, I do not know how long I have left.

L.B.

After the three read the page that A'lex kept safe for decades over and over again, it was time for the captain to wake up. No more time to play dead or even less to really be dying. They shut all the doors behind them and closed the curtains of all the windows in the house. Everyone turned off their mind projectors.

'Capitan Pig is still lost. How do you expect us to go forward without him?' Chekhovich argued.

'We have to do something!' Marxim said.

'Everything we have is circumstantial. Capitan Pig is still lost, and I am hungry. I want to go,' said Lucretia with arms crossed like a capricious child.

'How can you be so selfish?' Chekhovich mumbled.

Lucretia shrugged her shoulders, 'I have tried to help, but at this point, I'm tired. You promised me the best adventure of my life, but I feel I am in this alone. I am the one who makes the mess, the one that cleans the mess. The one that finds the clues and the one that fucks the people to get the clues. I mean, you expect me to put a broom up my ass and sweep the floor as well?'

In the dimly lit kitchen, a funeral silence was alternating with ferocious discussions, and finally, the group decided the fate of Captain Grunter.

Marxim proposed to wait, 'It's risky, but if we can get more information maybe …'

'Hospital!' Chekhovich said, ignoring the fact that as soon as the news of the captain being dead, dying, or something else came out, it would have definitely caused some kind of retaliation; the last one after being ignored for so long just wanted to get it over with.

Lucretia and Chekhovich had been there only for a few hours and already wanted to eliminate the problem. But Marxim had been holding the captain in his arms for days. He had not gotten up to eat, sleep, or piss. Watching Lucretia and Chekhovich fighting and screaming over and over was like walking in a cornfield and getting wounded by those sharp, mean leaves. He closed his eyes and tried to space out, but those leaves cut even when you stay still.

PER FAS
ET NEFAS

Captain Grunter was still trapped in A'lex's mind. In that vortex of darkness, cotton candy windows sporadically popped up during his descent into the void. Getting a hold of these was close to impossible. In these windows, memories of A'lex's life played out. Before he plunged into the bottomless pit of his existence, the captain managed to swing inside one of the windows. Immediately, he was catapulted through time, back to when A'lex was still a sweet, curled-hair child that was only guilty of cake murder and steak abuse. Abruptly, the captain plummeted onto a marble pavement. He looked around. He was in a corridor. He could smell truffle oil, coriander, and fresh fish. He wondered whether he was in a restaurant. For a moment, he forgot about his nightmare and stopped to enjoy the harmony of the food being cooked. A'lex, who wore a three-piece sailor suit in white and navy blue, sat on a chair at the end of the corridor. He gave distracted looks to the adjacent room. In there was a round glass office. Around 50 people sat around a pink marble table – its veins travelled from one side to the other and connected every part to the whole. Its legs were elaborated with capitals and decorated with acanthus leaves and scrolls. The oval room was a Baroque heaven. Golden curls of stucco mouldings climbed the dome in the form of a firmament with white and grey clouds from which a blue sky appeared and formed ornamental rods converging to the centre. From there, descended a rose gold chandelier à la Louis XIV with pendants of rock diamond, ruby, and emeralds, all of which were proudly stolen from South America and Africa.

It was hard to say exactly how many people were in the room because everyone looked and dressed the same: blacks, whites, yellows and browns, and all the other beautiful shades. They all looked the same. Even the women looked like the men. They all wore black, white, and red. All of them had small eyes and devilish smiles.

One of the men sitting next to another in black and in front of the one in black and red cleared his throat and stood up with dignified professionality. 'As we are all aware of why we are here today, I believe it would be more appropriate if we went straight into planning our next moves and skip the rituals.'

The other men around the table looked horrified. An ensemble of comments echoed in the oval room.

'Skip the rituals? What is this now?'

'Aren't we people anymore?'

'What's wrong? Do you have something better to do?'

'No rituals? Are we men or pigs?'

The murmur in the room became deafening.

'There, there. Now settle down, gentlemen.' A man dressed entirely in white walked around the table. His celestial aura and calming voice sedated the disorder. The man looked as if he had just descended from the sky painted on the ceiling. With angelic grace, he walked around the room and stopped in front of the man who had talked in his absence. 'You may have perhaps underestimated the symbolic importance of the game, dear Ceteary. Please, ladies and gentlemen … get in position.'

The White One now walked to the music station. 'Remember to wait for my command.'

The people got up from their seats and placed themselves in two lines, one in front of the other. The White One pointed his little finger right and left, and the two rows bowed at each other. Mozart, Violin Sonata No. 17 in C, K. 296 accompanied the gentlemen moving forward and shaking hands. They started exchanging pleasantries.

'Warm enough for you?'

'Sure is. Looks like rain, though.'

'Well, take care of yourself.'

'And you.'

Like in a speed dating contest, when the procedure had reached its peak, the participants, in an orderly fashion, passed onto the next guest.

'Well, you sure look fine.'

'And how's your family? All good?'

'It has been way too long!'

'Great, glad to see you again.'

'So long.'

'Don't be a stranger!'

After 15 minutes of empty conversations, smiles, and nodding, the music finally stopped, and the guests walked back to their seats. As soon as they sat down, not, a smile could be seen in the room.

'So.' The White One cleared his throat. 'As Ceteary mentioned before, we all know why we are here: to discuss the future of our nations. We, as a collective, must finally give something back to our people. Let me be clear, we are still unbeatable, sure, but things are not looking well. I have been cruising Twitter. Yes, people sharing, commenting, worst of all, thinking, and memes! Memes drenched in rebellious rhetoric everywhere. No, don't look at me like that, these memes are funny, and everything funny is potentially dangerous. As things are now, even a simple 'Hit Me Baby One More Time' Flash mob could potentially be the spark that will cause our overturn. Needless to mention that after last week's beating of protesters, journalists, legal observers, and medics in over 40 states, people are a bit bummed out. Tear gas, pepper spray, rubber bullets. Damn guys, what did you expect?'

'Pardon me, but protesters are always gonna protest,' one said.

'Don't get me wrong. I am not saying thou shall not beat and kill; I am saying don't be so obsolete. We are in the 21st century. Everyone is on their damned phone all the time, especially on these occasions.' The White One sat on the table yet spoke to those under him as equals. 'These kinds of videos are as viral as Covid-22. So, now you make a decision. Either stay a fossil, keep beating your people and broadcast it to the world, or take the better way. Think of the stick and the carrot. Let's keep them happy for a bit.'

'Happy?' a very unimpressed face exclaimed.

'Must we?' another one said.

'Well, not too happy, I'm sure,' another one tried to mediate, looking to The White One as a lost puppy.

'I hope you don't mean them ALL.'

'We can't keep them all happy, can we?'

'Look, the last few 'projects' have almost mined the entire future of humanity. I am not saying that your Chickenocide wasn't a brilliant idea, dear Ross; it was a great idea, followed by the enlighted campaign of the Bacon Wave. Thank you again, Miss Olligrom. And what is there to say about the avocado plan but: genius!'

Every time each member was congratulated, they shrugged their shoulders in fake modesty as if they just did their job and didn't need any praise or raise.

'Great ideas, ladies and gentlemen; you are all geniuses. But I didn't call you here to blow you and call you baby. Those were great ideas but with poor execution. The timing of these initiatives has been more than suspicious, and many of our citizens are realising it.'

'Well then, let's repress them. We haven't done the dictatorship thing for a while.'

'I appreciate the enthusiasm, I do. However, what we actually need is something bigger, something really revolutionary. We can't silence them all; we'd end up being the only humans on the planet.'

'Where do I sign up for that?' a bloated bald man said, almost choking on his laughter.

The White One smiled too. 'And who would take care of your dirty underwear, Toposky? I don't think anyone in this room would do that for you, not even Salvinee, who's so fond of organic matter!' He placated the laughing room. 'Nothing special, but we must give them something to take their minds away from the big bad wolf. So, tell me now, what is it that people need?'

'Well, that is such a broad question. I believe you cannot answer this query unless you analyse each country socially, environmentally, economically,' a woman said while others nodded with curled lips.

'Exactly. My people, for example, need water. But I gotta say, I am not too inclined to–'

'I believe my county needs hospitals or no wait, was it schools? I don't know, whatever. The point is, I am not going just to give them what they want. I mean, who am I? The–'

'Exactly,' the White One interrupted him, 'who are you?'

The man stood up with a little jump. 'President Achan, from Ngōn Bay.'

'I see. Ah, Ngōn Bay, beautiful! But yes, you are completely right. Why would a president build any kind of infrastructure in a country where the highest share of its population is rats?'

'Ahem, ratatouille,' someone in the back murmured.

Everyone at the round table laughed. President Achan sat down embarrassed, red on his round cheeks.

'So, let's spit-ball, guys. Let's talk rights, and damn, I can't believe I am saying this, let's talk equality. What can we offer our people to keep them tame?'

The guests looked left and right with eyes full of hope in the room, waiting for someone to speak up.

The White One started to clink his fingertips on the table. The noise of his long nails incited the men to start thinking and fast. The murmuring started again.

'Every country has both women and men, right? How about we give them the same rights?'

Everybody laughed, and the women laughed louder. One said, 'Come on, we need something that won't make people question our actions.'

'Let's decrease taxes,' one said, and another one laughed.

'Damn, since when did Italianos even pay taxes anyway?'

Everybody laughed.

'Let's … stop environmental damages.'

'No, that's too long term.'

'Let's end human trafficking.'

'But I was just gonna order a new baby wife.'

'Wait, I got a good one. Let's stop the cartels.'

'Yeah, we should start by putting you behind bars!' a woman said, giving a friendly pat to the man sitting next to her.

The White One got up. He was both amused and exasperated by their stupid naivety. 'Guys, can you stay serious for ten minutes? Only ten minutes. That's how much time we need to decide the future of the world.'

'I got one.' Someone from the back of the room stood up from their seat. 'I got one, Sir. I think it's a really good one.'

The White One had never heard or seen this mysterious person in the back.

'I think I know what it is that people need.'

'Please, go on.'

'What's more essential than bread, than water, than the internet itself? What is it that people crave more than love, more than family, more than …'

'Oh my, please, let's get this sermon over with and get to the point, will ya?'

'People need to know that they are better than others. Well, better than someone else, at least. They need to know that someone is doing worse than them, someone has less than them. Someone less "worthy." They need someone to hate.'

'Well, they already hate us.'

'Yes, but we are obviously better than them, and they know it. They hate us because …'

'Let's hear it. Why do they hate us?'

'They hate us because they ain't us, Sir.'

The White One touched his sharp-pointed goatee and gestured with his hand for the eager speaker to continue the theory.

'They need to hate someone close to them. Their neighbour, their teacher, I don't know … the postman. Someone they can directly hurt.'

'Haven't we carried the racist thing for long enough?'

'Yes, sir, but what if instead of race, we use class as a matrix? Every country has the rich and the poor.'

It didn't take much persuasion. 'That's a good point. Not incredibly original but acceptable,' a bearded man murmured to the one next to him.

'Well, then, I believe we have a winner … who's this gorgeous lady with brilliant ideas and–'

'Ladyboy–'

'Ahem … pardon me. I didn't mean to …'

Lady Boyce was glorious and taller than most of the people in the room. Her Ariana Grande ponytail let her caramel curls fall like a cascade on her wide and powerful shoulders. Her body looked as hard as steel, and the black suit she wore fell straight down her body without diminishing any of her curves. Her long and elegant hand fixed the hair behind her little ears and proudly showed an Adam's apple on her sensual Modigliano neck.

The lady smiled, poised and gracious. 'My name is Lady Boyce.'

Her face was a Spring of Botticelli. Her eyes, brown and yellow, were of the same shade as the nude lipstick on her voluptuous lips.

Everyone got up, obscuring Lady Boyce. They cheered and glorified each other for the hard work they just did.

Before they had the chance to grab the stem glasses in front of them, The White One cleared his throat, and everybody sat down again.

'Before we start the ceremonial fellatio ad invicem, I need the dates for the first edification on Paradise Island.'

'Our experts recommend we wait until Summer 2023. The rising temperature will help with the sedimentation and fertilisation of the soil, as well as other things I don't need to bore you with. This will also give us time to deal with PR. I have already assigned the task to my specialists, and they will get back to me with drafts and stats by the end of the week.'

'Yes, our polls show us that the overcrowding of the major capitals will be optimal next year to promote the financial incentive to both prospective buyers and tenants.'

'Oh, I thought maybe we could start to move some call centres down there. Just to test the stability and safety of the island,' said the man next to Lady Boyce – a man with piercing blue eyes. The kind of blue you should never trust. He had a dark brown handlebar moustache. In the upwardly curved extremities of the moustache, crumbs of his lunch tried to escape. The trap was particularly lengthy and intricate. Without his compassionate and confident stroke, the crumbs would have stayed there forever. He sat on his swivel chair like he had no spine.

'I hope you are kidding me. First and foremost, think. A dump with make-up is still a dump, dear Strontsky. We don't want working-class crap to be the first thing buyers see, do we? You must realise this gives the wrong message. Yes, an island in the Pacific sounds heavenly, but let's remember it's still a trash island! Trash people doing trash jobs, living on a trash island. No, no, what we need instead are young professionals, yoga instructors, visual artists.' The White One always knew what was best.

'Vegans!' DüMal nodded.

'Absolutely, Dümal, well said.'

'You are right; I wasn't thinking clearly,' the man mumbled, adjusting his posture on the chair.

'Very well then.' The White One took a break to pour champagne into his stem glass. 'I believe we can finally start the celebrations. I am proud of you, my friends. I believe we are off to a great new era. And welcome to the new member of the team, Lady Boyce.' The White One raised his glass in her direction.

'It's a privilege to be amongst you,' she said.

'Oh no, believe me, the privilege is all mine,' the White One replied.

The opening of hundreds of zips echoed outside the room where the little A'lex stood, still unimpressed and bored. Captain Grunter looked at the kid who waited in his dashing outfit. He felt bad about the handsome little sailor in navy blue who never really had a chance at not being an asshole. The captain's compassion didn't last long. The floor started to shake. It was time to go. The sand-coloured walls began to melt as the memory started disintegrating again. The captain jumped on A'lex's lap and closed his eyes, hoping to escape the darkness that was about to swallow him. The memory disappeared until he saw only scattered images. He saw A'lex's first kiss, a boy whose pink skin reminded him of a sausage; a green door; his hands interlocking with Lucretia amid a passionate night; his hands interlocking with others – hundreds of people; a green door opening; an unopened present little A'lex kicked into the fire; millions of sunsets; the rain falling on his estate in London; the ecstasy of his best nights in Ibiza, sweating over strangers and laughing at the futility of life. Then just darkness.

Everything that ever mattered to A'lex was erased.

***

As the lovers shouted at each other, the walls around Marxim crumbled. The windows shuttered, and fire destroyed everything in his panicked haze of fear, anger, and sadness.

Then a finger. Some hope.

Then silence.

'Oink,' Captain Grunter screamed. Marxim's eyes turned nuclear green, and he started talking as if he was possessed. He kept repeating an address. 170 Old Montague Street E15NA. 170 Old Montague Street E15NA.

Captain Grunter opened his gentle eyes. Marxim was normal again, and on his face, both shame and happiness mixed in an unstoppable stream of tears. He caressed the captain, who didn't back away from the infamous finger. He oinked and grunted and shook his curly little tail. Everything would be fine, and although A'lex was still catatonic, life was beautiful.

DEPRESSIONISM AND NOSTALGIA

170 Old Montague Street, E15NA, was just a few blocks down from Lucretia's house. Outside, a fresh breeze whispered on Chekhovich's neck as he analysed the derelict building he was about to enter. In front of him was a three-storey house with decaying beige paint. Only a green door between him and the secrets of contemporary history. On the rusty handle of the door, a necklace hung. Although most of its once white pearls and greenstones were ruined, the necklace still held some of its charms. Chekhovich was hesitant and stood on the threshold for a few cowardly seconds after he unlocked the door. Marxim, intrepid and empathising with the deteriorating appearance of the building, barged right in, shoving Chekhovich to the side. As they walked inside the house, a putrid smell of humidity and mould hit their nostrils, lingering on the surface of the

linoleum floor. To their left, a collapsed staircase made it impossible for them to go up. Ahead, they found the kitchen, one of those cheap, light brown MDF cabinet units, the ones specifically built for the poor. In a world where everything was cheap, people still needed to differentiate the poor from the poorer, and so, landlords installed these horrid lines of furniture in their proprieties – a little way to keep the tenants humble.

Chekhovich opened a cabinet. Empty, as he expected. After the kitchen, there was a small garden where weeds grew wild and free in the small rectangular area allowed to nature. Cement and wood divided the microcosm from the neighbours' dominion. The two went back to the kitchen with nowhere else to go and sat on a synthetic leather couch with cushions worn out by millions of asses. They waited on Lucretia, who was using her dog as an excuse to spend most of the morning chilling on the bed and taking selfies. As they waited, the smell of humidity seemed to latch onto their skin.

***

Lucretia entered the kitchen talking on the phone with a girl she met at work, Sophie. 'We got to his house and had more drinks, more—yes, then I touched his head, and all of a sudden, he got all serious.'

Sophie was not really important. Not because she wasn't hot or because she didn't earn a lot, but mostly because she was one of those interchangeable office girls: Sarah, Jessica, or Sophie – all blonde and blue-eyed. The office girls not only looked like each other but also behaved the same. They wore formal clothes, kinda sexy, kinda boring, and they thought they made it in life. They got their coffees from those family-style franchises and always sent back their order if it was not up to their instagrammable standards. Smiling while complaining made them feel like they were not doing anything wrong. After all, they paid £2.50 for their drinks, and the price certainly included the dignity of the barista.

Marxim and Chekhovich stared at Lucretia.

'Ahem, he said he needed to tell me something: I like you very much blah blah blah, I never say this to other girls, you are special, you got big boobs, I feel like I can trust you, we can build something meaningful here, and lol, he keeps on talking about the same things. A future together, honesty blah blah. I have a hair piece—'

'What?' the girl on the other side of the phone screamed. 'Herpes?'

'If only that were the case.'

'Uh-hhh,' the girl said, utterly disgusted.

'What do you mean, ugh, don't you have it? Anyway, no, the guy has a hairpiece. You really can't trust anyone these days … Yes, I know, right? No, of course. If … Well, yes, I do. Ah, OK, so being bald is fine, but having an adventurous disease is not. No, not a disease, a condition. Would you shame someone for having asthma? You should be fucking ashamed of yourself, Soph-Sarah. Everyone that matters has herpes, you hear me? Everyone!'

Chekhovich clawed at the phone and immediately backed away. 'Stop wasting time; we got stuff to do.'

'Like what?' She looked around. 'Home makeover is not really my thing; maybe Marxim could help you.'

'Oh well, I have built my own farm ...' he said proudly. 'Stop being so anal. Why are you always like this?' 'Anal? Me?' Lucretia started opening the cabinets, hoping to find anything to throw at Chekhovich. She was irritated by the fact that the cabinets were empty.

'There's nothing there. Try your luck elsewhere,' Chekhovich said, and he was right.

The first two cabinets were empty. She kept opening and slamming the cabinets, all predictably empty. Finally, she found a full one. An overflowing quantity of papers and reports fell on the floor.

'So, you checked already, did you, Chekhovich?' Lucretia said, opening the rest of the cabinets with the ardour of discovery.

Chekhovich began opening all the other drawers and cupboards he didn't think of inspecting before. They left Marxim to the trouble of picking up the files from the floor. Between gaps and creaking bones, he managed to put everything on the dusty and sticky table. The other two kept racing to inspect anything that could be opened – fridge, freezer, even the toilet. Marxim started reading the documents. Lucretia unsuccessfully tried climbing the rubble of the staircase and went back to the kitchen, filthy but smug.

'So, you were waiting for me to do this?' she said, cleaning the dust off her face.

'What do you think these are?' asked Marxim, reading the papers that made little sense to him.

'Well, we got some coffee to brew ...' said Chekhovich, ecstatic. He had always loved homework.

'Can't we just ask the captain to bring us some?'

Lucretia asked Chekhovich.

'He's busy checking the oxygen levels,' Marxim answered, browsing the files, and looking at Lucretia sideways. 'Better not bother him.'

'Oh, come on, he must be flying over so many artisanal coffee shops right now. I can already smell the aroma. Please, it just takes a …'

'Oh, my Manson, grow up! Come to the table,' Chekhovich shouted.

'Come to the table,' she repeated in her most childish voice.

'Listen to this, guys,' Marxim continued. 'The advent of digital mental disorders.'

Proposal N13

The Depressionism

By

Harfonzer DüMal
DO YOU HAVE A MENTAL DISORDER?
AND IF YOU DON'T, WHY?

Depression Manifesto

We are the Revolution. We are depressed, repressed, anxious, bipolar, schizophrenic, and bored. We are teachers, doctors, leaders, brands, tourists, immigrants, and influencers. We are the industry and the public. We are world citizens. We are a movement and a community. We are you.

We love life. But we don't want your rules to exploit our lifestyle and destroy our comfort. We demand radical, revolutionary change.

- **#1** Depressionism wants society to provide us with dignified work, from home and in pyjamas. Work that does not enslave, endanger, exploit, overwork, harass, abuse, or discriminate against anyone, but mostly me. Depressionism liberates the worker and empowers the human to stand up for their rights.

- **#2** Depressionism provides fair and equal rights. It enriches the livelihood of everyone working or not, in and outside the bedroom. Depressionism lifts people out of sadness, creates thriving victims, and fulfils aspiration.

- **#3** Depressionism gives people a voice, making it possible to speak and pick up calls without fear.

- **#4** Depressionism respects culture and heritage. Depressionism is always appropriate but never appropriates, although everything is fair in love and war.

- **#5** Depressionism stands for solidarity, inclusiveness, and democracy, regardless of race, class, gender, age, shape, or ability. It champions diversity as crucial for success. But only for those inside the movements, the others can and should fuck off.

- **#6** Modern society destroys our souls, depletes our precious resources, degrades us, and pollutes our thoughts. Depressionism mindfully redesigns, recuperates, and restores humanity by giving up.

- **#8** Depressionism is transparent and accountable. We account everyone else for our misfortunes, mistakes, misadventures. We embrace errors as part of our path and blame society for them.

- **#9** Depressionism measures success by how many hours you spend in bed and how many series you watch on Netflix. Depressionism places equal value on financial loss, online shopping, and human well-being, measured in the number of happy pills taken.

- **#10** Depressionism lives to express, reflect, protest, discomfort, commiserate, and share.

Chekhovich thought about his childhood, which was not completely awful, just the right amount of sadness that he could use to justify his shitty behaviour. His mother killed herself, so that was a bonus. His father's grave voice resonated in his head. 'Where are your pills? Take them now!' His mother's cry haunted him, her voice full of sorrow and disappointment: 'Why is your room always so dirty?' Chekhovich felt his mother's heartbreak each time she would enter his room. He felt the fire on his cheeks that accompanied each of his father's shouts after his mother's death.

'What have I just read?' asked Marxim, scratching his head.

Chekhovich banged his hands on the table, blankly staring at the wall in front of him. 'I was only a child when I got it – the Depression 2025. It was the only thing that got me through childhood. Were my parents ashamed of me? Obviously. Every day was a war in my house. My mother bombarding me with questions: what would you like for breakfast? How are you? What are you gonna do today? Do you want to do something together? I can take you here, and I can take you there!'

'Well, they sound like they cared about you.'

Chekhovich ignored Marxim's words. 'Why can't you be different, love? She'd ask me. Mom, I can't be different! I am just indifferent to everything. I tried telling her, but she never really understood my struggle. They gave me happy pills and complained they didn't work, gave me chores, and complained I didn't do them. Of course, I didn't do them. I was just their little broken boy. But did they ever try to understand me? How many times I wanted to eat a freaking pizza, and I couldn't because talking on the phone gave me anxiety.'

Lucretia and Marxim looked at Chekhovich as one would look at a person pleading 'all lives matter.'

'I had social anxiety, major depression disorder, and minor depression disorder.'

'A mild retardation?' Lucretia whispered to Marxim.

'A doctor on the internet diagnosed me. Ah, and I also have – I mean, had suicidal thoughts. Got that from my mother's side along with high blood pressure.'

'So what? Do you want to be sanctified? Maybe put in one of those facilities they sent depressionists?' Lucretia asked, irritated and unforgiving.

'What? They were not facilities. They were communities where everyone was free to wear pyjamas all day,' Chekhovich said, getting defensive.

'Goddamit! What's there to be so depressed about in your life? Have you seen what happened to Captain Grunter? Did he complain once? Did he get suicidal thoughts?'

'If he ever does, we are gonna have a nice dinner though, right?' Lucretia asked and looked around for approval. Everybody nodded.

'Of course, we are, but anyway, this is not a competition on whose pain is more acceptable or virtuous. I just wanted them to treat me like everybody else, but better obviously, because I was different, and when I wanted to eat a freaking pizza, somebody should have called the restaurant for me. Is that too much to ask?'

Marxim was irritated by Chekhovich's self-indulgence.

'I think you are completely right, Marxim, but I completely understand those who are depressed because what's not to be depressed about in this life? I don't have one depressed bone in my body, and I have never thought of suicide, but I don't judge who does, and I have to say, I am definitely open to all experiences. Never say never, right?'

Chekhovich was impressed by Lucretia's deep and sensible understanding of the issue. Not being patronised for once in his life made his dick so strong for a moment, he felt that he didn't need his enhancer anymore.

'Whatever, let's just keep looking,' Marxim grunted with his face buried in dusty files.

'My turn,' announced Lucretia with authority, 'I think I got something interesting.' She cleared her throat.

Proposal N37

Operation Nostalgia

By

Connor Osumbor

Don't you miss the time when starving children in Africa were just an excuse to make your kids finish their fucking broccoli?

"Do you miss the time when being happy was so easy? When you didn't have to watch savethechildrenz adverts showing sorrowful starving children at dinner time, just when you were about to devour your wholesome Sunday roast? A time when you could keep the lights on in your house without having an environmentalist knocking at your door asking how you feel about knowing your bathroom light bulb is killing fishes? A time when you didn't even need to learn how electricity is produced because every day you came back home from a long day at the office, and that's how electricity is produced, thanks to your hard work! Don't you miss the time when you didn't have to feel guilty about buying your 3rd house? When at parties, people only spoke of the local top slut and not the war in Chile? The times when there was less useless information, and you didn't need to pretend to care and know everything that was happening in the world?

I do. I miss that, my friends. Nowadays, we are the silent victims of bully-like pressure on social media. If you don't share a link about the inhuman condition of factory workers in Romania, you are insensible. If you share too many, you are a plotter, a commie, a bored intellectual sharing equity links from his £2000 laptop. Left, right, whatever, there's no answer or action good enough to silence those voices in your head and the voices around you trying to make you feel guilty about things you have rightfully earned, or even better, <u>inherited</u>.

We acknowledge your confusion, beautify your pain, and, more than that, erase any discomfort modern society imposes on you, for it's hard to find balance. Come with me to a new old world where you don't have to lose your mind and waste hours choosing what to watch on Netflix. We know what you want in this world, and we will give it to you <u>when we want</u>. Rediscover the pleasure and the eagerness of watching an old movie on TV. Reclaim the anger and the drama coming from missing your favourite movie due to a TV breakdown. We offer you the chance of rediscovering life in its most unique attribute, unrepeatability. We offer you a broadcast programme that includes family masterpieces like Titanic, Terminator, and Toy Story. A world in which girls always shave their armpits and boys don't wear fishnets–"

'Wow, that sounds boring,' said Lucretia, throwing the paper back in the midst.

'I think my parents were big 90s supporters,' murmured Chekhovich, thinking about his parents' matching F.R.I.E.N.D.S. sweatshirts.

'Of course, everyone was. Indifference towards the environment, cheap everything everywhere,' continued Lucretia.

'Absolutely, but also the sense of wonder,' Marxim said with sparkling eyes. 'I was born in 1975. I have witnessed the four big transformations: the phone, the internet, the Bacon Wave, and The Great Avocado War. I have seen everything and done enough, and I can tell you guys, the 90s were the time to live it up! People were looking forward to life, dreaming about the technological progress that was slowly arriving. Sure, we only had phones and computers, but we felt like we were living in an ultra-sophisticated modern reality. Of course, a war here and there, but also technology, economy, arts, music. Everything was booming. Children in the 90s were so very happy. There were video games, Dragon Ball, Digimons, Pokemons … And better than anything else, great TV commercials …'

Marxim's mind record played the advertisement of *Cuddles*, a fabric conditioner that "smelled like heaven-fresh cotton-apricot." In the ad, two children ran around their mama, who happily indulged in their kids' fun while hanging the laundry without skipping a beat. The father, a handsome man, gazed from afar at his wholesome family. Pride and love, *Cuddles*; the best product for the best family.

Marxim turned off his mind recorder, and his tone suddenly changed. 'Then the 2000s came, the sense of marvel started to disappear. I don't know why it did, perhaps because the prediction of the apocalypse failed to come or maybe, just because. Things evolved so drastically. Although the internet began with a great start, with people spending their time gathering information and connecting intellectually, socially, culturally … it inevitably ended up being used just to hook up.'

'Marxim, was the Depressionism before or after the Bacon Wave?' Chekhovich asked, trying to create a timeline of the documents they found to see if they connected in any way.

Marxim wasn't sure and pretended not to hear the question. He went to the toilet instead, to think.

The truth was that the Depressionism was impossible to date.

It took an enormous amount of time and a shared effort to put the Depressionism in action. Some might have said it was the biggest social operation ever put in place. It took almost 100 years to pollute the air enough to influence the mental health of the citizens. It took around 70 years to produce enough material to ensure that most children grew up around trash and malodorous garbage. Then 200 years of hard work to cause the warming effect and the subsequent shift of the weather conditions thoroughly generated to wear people down and boost depression levels. It was an eternity of inaccessible architecture accompanied by the constant electoral propaganda, which promised the destruction of architectural barriers and a world where disabled people wouldn't feel excluded. Soon, politicians realised that once they did amend the barriers and granted the disabled the chance to move around easily, they would have had to work properly to keep those votes. And at the same time, if they didn't give these people the chance to move freely, they would lose those votes anyway. So, they just stopped promising and focused on the audiences easier to charm. Three hundred years of inaccessible bureaucracy made people feel unable to do anything. Wasting precious hours of their life filling out futile, never-ending forms nobody would ever read and completing interminable job applications even for the most practical of jobs. Lie-based cover letters, skill competencies, culture-fit assessments, personality tests, and extreme makeovers were the standard process for applying for a job – any job from tech to hospitality.

The cherry on top came in the mid-90s. The internet originated a stream of hyper-information, which had suddenly made people capable of comprehending not only theirs but other people's struggles. Although people could virtually find the answer to everything in cyberspace and free themselves from the constructs of the world they had been taught, users mostly ended up finding sources that legitimised their beliefs. Their research was tailored around their tastes and dislikes. The internet mirrored what they experienced in their analogic life, a false consensus effect that made them assume their behaviour was the logical one and think that everyone would automatically behave in the same way in certain circumstances. For example, the average Luigi believed that pineapple did not go on pizza; he surrounded himself with others of the same creed and ignored the possibility that some degenerate and avant-gardist kept ordering in the flat next door sanctifying this aberration to the world. Like in real life, on the internet, people sought out groups of others similar to them, those that could reinforce their perception of reality.

In real life, girls went into the bathroom with girls that shared their tampon size and lipstick shade and guys … well, guys who hung out together, raped together.

However, unlike real life, where everyday people were forced to interact with others of different status, race, and political views, on the internet, it was way too easy to lose the perception of reality and wallow in their personal beliefs.

The challenge of self-identity in cyberspace was a thin line between fake news and clickbait trying to seduce you into populist temptations and a kind of delusional, self-fulfilling prophecy. Always "one click away" from saving the world by putting our names on the Avaaz online petition and constantly receiving emails about even more terrifying events, you could have never stopped. This was optimal to create the frustration and isolation that the Depressionism was based on.

The internet – Depressionist pride and joy created an entropy of information that hit its users like an erupting volcano. How could people have been happy sipping their fish-matcha-latte when on their phone, a girl was being decapitated, and a man suffocated to death? How could people go on with their day after watching the videos of nuclear explosions, hurricanes destroying entire islands, and puppies being burned alive? All during their commute to work!

The chance of globalisation without destruction the internet promised ended up in a global depression. Understanding one's personal inability to do good without radically uprooting their life made the sensible ones feel worthless and gave the cold ones the certainty that some lives were worthless; just created to become viral videos and trauma porn. It started with a jumper, 'Cute but Lazy,' and ended up watching the ten seasons of Friends for the 5th time to numb the pain. When your device asked if you were still watching, looking at your soul reflected on the screen, in those three seconds of darkness, the fixations, fears, and disgust for everything humankind has done wrong were all brought back.

Most of the time, as soon as you pressed 'yes,' everything was forgotten, and again, you could go back to the biggest love story ever played – Ross and Rachel. However, there were times when not even the fact that they were on a break could make you forget about the wars, radiation, possible extinction, lack of natural resources, diseases, genocides, food crises, water, electricity, land, air, morals, values, and all the 'isms.' In that ocean of never-ending kitten videos, infidels whose throats were cut on live-stream, likes, comments, and download culture, politics, and life meshed, blurring the line between what was real and what was realer.

However, the enchantment and entanglement in the internet assemblage did not only create mindless masses of slaves complicit in their own commercial and ideological exploitation, it was also an anthropogenic medium. It built a new kind of citizen capable of canalising forces from virtually all around the world, and it terrified the rotten class of politicians governing the Earth.

Right?

Marxim flushed the toilet and completely lost his train of thought.

'What about Operation Nostalgia? Tell us more!' Lucretia said to Marxim. She and Chekhovich were hanging onto every word from his lips.

'I guess things were not looking up anymore. The 90s was the last decade when people still dreamt up. So, they recycled it.' Marxim was elated with his new position.

'Why do you think they did this? Recycling an era, I mean,' Chekhovich asked.

'Why do you think anyone does anything? They probably had too many warehouses full of unsold and useless "vintage" things, so they made them "great again,"' Lucretia answered.

'Have you found anything connected with A'lex's memory?' Marxim added, holding his face, which felt like a boulder between his hands.

'The plan of that Lady Boyce, you mean? I have checked everywhere, but I couldn't find anything linking to a "hate plan,"' Chekhovich answered, turning the pages of the reports in front of him.

'What about the White One? Anything about him in your files?'

'Nope,' Chekhovich and Lucretia answered in unison.

'Should we … maybe ask the captain to go back into A'lex's head?' Lucretia mumbled.

Marxim suddenly stood up, angry and offended by the thought. 'We almost lost him last time. What are you talking about?'

'Yeah, but without any progress on this, we're lost anyway,' Lucretia answered.

'Look at all the stuff we have here. Get off your asses and keep reading instead of trying to find an easier path. Back in my time, we didn't have mind searchers. We had to type everything we wanted – go back and forth between browsers, accept cookies, and get viruses. You know nothing about hard work,' Marxim shouted, angrily pushing his chair away from the table and turning towards the window. He contemplated the unkempt garden until he finally heard his two companions going through the papers again. It was getting darker now. The last rays of sunlight gave their final nurturing touch to the weeds and nettles. Marxim was hungry.

How many piles would they have to look into? Who could guarantee they would even find anything useful at all? In this world that rewarded short-sightedness and deafness, why even try to challenge the status quo – for free and in your own precious free time? These were the questions that lingered in the younger generation's minds. Meanwhile, Marxim, resolute and motivated not to put his son's health at risk, sat again and began to read and highlight every document, every note, and every email address he found.

'Oh, my Manson, can you imagine doing homework like that? Lol,' Lucretia whispered to Ceko.

'Manson …' Chekhovich's beautiful mind went into overdrive. 'What if …' he mumbled, making meaningless sounds and motions with his big, crazy eyes. Everybody expected a big revelation was coming at any moment.

'What if Manson is the White One?'

'Everyone knows that Manson is dead,' Marxim answered, disappointed.

'And I am not feeling too well either!' Lucretia said, exchanging an understanding glance with Marxim.

'Can you be serious for once?'

'No, I don't think so, Ceko, but also no, I don't think Manson is the white guy. There's no connection, no proof that would make me believe that,' answered Lucretia. 'How about Strontsky instead? He's a hyper-villain, he must know something, and he's local. How about we leave this shit to dust over and rot and go to him instead? The captain could easily get into his … never mind. I mean, we could go and just ask him a couple of questions. I am sure I can get something out of him,' Lucretia said with fake modesty.

'That is not the kind of business we are conducting here,' Chekhovich replied.

'You know what, guys? I agree, but no mind searching. The captain needs to rest. Let's just go and see him and interview him. Ceko, you are some sort of writer, right? You, Lucretia, you have all the connections, all the brains. I have … I will squeeze him like a mussel.'

All of them salivated at the thought of cold, tart lemon-mussel juice, and off they went to the farm. Another day, another little tassel of the puzzle. As Lucretia slammed the door behind her, the white and green necklace swung. Chekhovich turned on the car, and everyone closed their doors. Marxim complained about having to fasten their seatbelts. Lucretia moaned about the windows not going down. Everyone criticised the music. In the meantime, upstairs between the rubble and dust, other pieces of truth laid unfound and forever forgotten.

LAST MAN WANKING

Once they arrived home, something that happened on the way changed everyone's mood. When they were around 30 minutes away from home, the smell of a rotten corpse broke the harmony between the three. Being a piece of shit car, all the windows were broken and unable to go down. Chekhovich, who couldn't bear to hear any more of Lucretia's comments about his piece of junk, and how you are what you drive, opened the AC. However, all the AC did was freshen up the fart fragrance. Chekhovich and Lucretia took it for granted, accusing the old and incontinent Marxim of dropping a Himmler on them. Marxim was maddened by the insult and argued that he was absolutely positive that Lucretia was the culprit. He felt outraged that only because she had a nice bum, she thought she could dump one whenever and wherever she wanted. That kind of entitlement was exactly what he hated about the new generations.

Chekhovich, around the end of the trip, began to think the offender might have actually been Lucretia. However, he refused to believe that her insides were as rotten as everyone else's. He liked to think that her internal organs were all hot, wet, and perky. Red, shiny, cherry flavoured blood flowed through her veins. It was really hard maintaining this vision immersed in the stench of the car, but Chekhovich was a romantic.

Lucretia did fart, it was true. But she did not fart before Marxim, and certainly, she only did it after Chekhovich. The deadly and persistent aroma was the result of all the egoistic needs. Neither of them wanted to confess.

After they arrived, Captain Grunter was still out on duty. A'lex came, wagging his little pink tail to welcome the humans. Nobody gave him any attention apart from Marxim, who scratched his rind and slapped his bum while A'lex twirled and jumped around him, still smelling of mould and farts. They ate in silence, and each went their own way.

To avoid everyone else, Lucretia went outside. She sat on the porch and looked at the purple sky silently extending to the horizon. Living in the city trained Lucretia to find comfort in the crashes and cries of urban life. Even before that, living with her parents, she learnt how to cling and cherish each noise; her mother's constant cough – which she was able to recognise from a distance – and her father's orchestral snoring that kept her up all night uncountable times. Now all this silence around her made her feel uneasy, empty. A'lex's grunts and blaring hoofs reassured her she was still alive. As Lucretia scratched the pig's back, she thought about when he was human. About his obnoxious way of asking her to do some 'extra unpaid hours' for the company's good, as if she was supposed to care about the company. She wondered if he missed her or anything from his old life.

Chekhovich went to the guest room and laid down on the bed. He was holding a book he could crack open at any time and pretend to read as soon as someone entered. After a couple of hours, he finally started reading 'A Spiderless House.' Chekhovich had always enjoyed reading, mainly as a performative activity, but he loved this book. He always carried it around with him and used it as inspiration. He enjoyed it so much, and he didn't need to read each sentence twice or skip pages – or pretend to get it. The book was classical vegan literature and treated him to incredibly trendy yet unconventional themes. It was a thriller about the threat of protein shakes in a world of inexistent spiritualism and 50 Shades of Grey kinks. Very gripping.

Marxim stayed at the table playing French cards, his only company. The dirty dishes were left on the table by his guests. Again, back in his time, this would not have happened. Probably.

He paced around the kitchen, looked outside the window, and nibbled snacks he wasn't craving. Marxim opened cabinets he knew he only used to store cleaning products or uninteresting items. He smelled tea bags. He had so many varieties, and he didn't even drink tea. He dreamed of desiring something so he could appease his wants. But unfortunately, he didn't want anything at all, and although this might feel like the ultimate freedom, it felt more like a tragedy. On the plastic marble of the kitchen, behind Chekhovich's denim backpack, he saw something an old flame sent him a couple of weeks ago before everything started. A red ribbon held a yellow paper wrap around the package and made it look luscious but homely, with a fake artisanal authenticity that was so hip years ago. The biscuits were raisin and rosemary. The former lover knew Marxim would have never eaten them. *Motherfucker,* he thought with a smile on his face. He untied and tied the ribbon until he thought it looked impeccable. Satisfied with his perfection, he went to sleep, time to rest.

* * *

Lucretia entered the kitchen after taking a nap under the portico and had a cold glass of water. The way the water freshened everything inside her made her feel alive, pure. She looked around and analysed the corners of the room. Nothing, in particular, she just liked how the apricot walls broke into one another with no end and no beginning. When she finally looked down, her eyes fell on an inviting red ribbon package. Without removing the ribbon, she took a sneak peek. The smell of its insides soon betrayed the pretty package. Lucretia put the cookies down immediately. She was relieved she didn't like them and was glad she was safe from the threat flour posed to her delicate intestines. No gluten today, she thought, proud of herself. But then, before she could even realise what she was doing, she snatched a piece of biscuit from under the wrap. With surgical precision and without ripping the paper, she threw the bit in her mouth. She hated herself; she knew she had to be strong for the day after. Her intestines held the future of the team. The last thing she needed was to run to the bathroom while all the action was happening. She looked left and right to check nobody was around and stealthily tossed the biscuits in the trash. She buried the package deep in the bin to cover the deed and adorned it with more garbage on top.

She got out of the kitchen knowing she accomplished something big, not only for herself but for the whole of humanity. Nothing would have minded her intestinal well-being, not tonight. Lucretia walked away, swaying her bum even if nobody was watching – that was actually when she gave her best hip action, tried new tempos and movements she would have then used when needed and wanted.

When she arrived at the guest room, from the ajar door, she saw Chekhovich sitting on the futon they had shared from that glorious first day they met. He was picking his poor eyebrows. He looked worried. Thinking? Planning? Probably just waiting for the night to be over. Lucretia wondered what was in that beautiful, dark-haired head of his, but then again, why? What was the point of sharing the last night together or looking into his gorgeous green-blue eyes and telling him everything was fine? Chekhovich was a boring fuck, and he would always be one. Although she liked torturing him and strongly believed she had the potential to possibly break his heart, she decided that leaving would have been better. They would never be the kind of couple that spends their nights simply being. They would never waste hours looking for the trashiest movies and hug endlessly, even on the hottest days of February. With him, it would have always been a competition between who could pretend to know more meaningless things, watching the most pretentious movies, drinking themselves into oblivion to forget their loneliness, and finding each other at the bottom of a shitty fuck. Additionally, Lucretia had a peculiar stupidity, the one martyrs have. By being with him, she would eventually sacrifice herself to save his confidence. At that point, no doubt, he would have dumped her because she was not challenging him enough anymore or maybe just because she got fatter. It's always these kinds of people that destroy you. Always those nerdy guys with round Harry Potter glasses and dimples. Those cute guys with small dicks are always the ones hiding the biggest egos. They always want someone better than them. Lucretia felt weird thinking that even those losers aspired for something they didn't deserve.

It happened before to her. That, for love and loneliness, she had endured boring conversation, forgiven boring sex and bad morning breath, and for what? How was she ever repaid? Those mediocre lovers despised themselves so much that as soon as they saw a beam of acceptance in someone else's eyes, they felt outraged, betrayed. "How could she sleep with me? How dare she love me?" How another person could see past the depths of their inadequacy was unbelievable to them. Therefore, when someone ignored or accepted their inferiority, they must have been even worse than them. So, bye-bye bitch.

Suddenly, the inspiring words of *Bad Bunny*, avant-garde poet of reggaeton, played in her head: "Yo Perreo Sola". She turned her shoulders to Chekhovich, left him downstairs alone in the abyss where he belonged, and stomped away on the staircase with no regrets – her Valkyrie posture empowering her. She found an empty room at the end of the grey felted carpet corridor and hoped it was not Marxim's room she was about to enter. She didn't want to send him the wrong message, a thing she was accused of constantly doing.

With her hand on the wall, she scouted for a light switch she never found. Sneaking in the dark room lit only by the silver reflection of the moon, she heard Marxim snoring through the walls. 'Noice,' she thought to herself as she threw the impalpable red satin shirt she wore all day on the floor. Undoing the lace of her sweatpants, she craved again those rosemary cookies she didn't even like, and for a split second, she considered going downstairs to save them from the jail of plastic and dirt she condemned them to.

No, no, no! She slapped her legs and took a deep breath; time to sleep now. She slipped under the cotton bedsheet that felt so fresh and flowery under her skin. She stretched her arms and yawned. Retracting her arms, she touched her breasts, feeling the trimmed lace of her bra under her fingertips. Her hands caressed her body and stopped on her hip, where she played with her hip bone and her culottes. She grabbed her pussy.

The door was wide open in less than a minute, and Captain Grunter stood at the threshold. He switched on the light comfortably positioned on the wall at his height – just 60cm up from the ground with his nose. Not expecting anyone in his room, he immediately backed away and turned the light off, making sure he would not disturb the Venus on his bed. He watched Lucretia looking at him as he cleaned his hoofs on the carpet. He did not know what to do. Lucretia held the bedsheet around her chest. Neither of them knew the etiquette to follow in these cases. Captain Grunter, who had just done the last rounds of oxygen checks in the city, was tired and just wanted to sleep. With his mouth, he pulled the bedsheet that hid Lucretia's beautiful body and stared at her, not like a pig but like an artist. Lucretia scooted over, and the captain jumped on the bed approaching her head with his nose. He kept looking at her, and she loved being looked at. It felt sexy, and it felt safe, like sending nudes to your gay best friend.

They kept staring at each other in silence until the captain fell asleep drooling on one side. Lucretia caressed his rind until she also felt the heaviness of the darkness closing in on her eyes.

* * *

Before the final night, Chekhovich was scared. He sat for endless hours on the bed he had shared with Lucretia since the beginning of this crazy, senseless story. He waited for her to come and join him. The long minutes followed one another. He hoped she would take his face in her hands and stop acting like such a bitch. He wasn't sure if it was acting or being. Then, while plucking his eyebrows, he heard her steps on the stairs and knew she would never come; she would never be what he needed, never stop being a bitch. Defeated and unsurprised, he went to the kitchen and was relieved when he found it empty yet dirty – that's when he gave his best. He took dishwasher soap and other detergents, slipped into Marxim's yellow plastic gloves, and started cleaning and scrubbing like a perfect 50s housewife.

He gathered all the items that didn't belong to the kitchen in a basket and cleared all the surfaces to be sprayed with an all-purpose cleaner. He ran the sink with hot soapy water and dropped all the dirty dishes and glasses in it. He felt unbearably lonely. He submerged his hands in hot water and focused on the green apple smell of the soap. He shut his eyes, inhaling and exhaling. He wanted to cry.

He scrubbed and washed and drained everything while keeping his tears captive in his sockets. He moved to the refrigerator, a mess that could maybe make him forget everything – his sadness, his loneliness, even his name. He cleaned all the shelves and dried the yellow, sticky water on the bottom of the compartments. He threw away what looked like cottage cheese in a milk bottle and other rotten items still wrapped in plastic as the day they were bought. He saw a silky red ribbon in the trash, the same red as Lucretia's satin shirt. He shoved it deeper in the bin, punched it until the garbage was completely compressed in the cylindrical shape of the bucket. He closed the bag and put it outside for the trash people to pick up the following day. Chekhovich swept the floor and turned off the lights. Everything was clean, and everything would be fine.

He remembered what his mommy told him countless times, even on that far away September day before she killed herself: 'Everything is cleaned, and everything will be fine.' For a short second, he wondered if it was all that cleaning that killed his mother, all the pressure from keeping the house clean at all times, and the inability to do so because living was dirty. He went to sleep but left the door ajar in case Lucretia had a change of heart and wanted to cuddle and hump later in the night, and in case she didn't, he put on his pants enhancer on the 'fuck yes' function.

***

The night was electric, and Marxim was still feeling lonely and anxious. The idea of not knowing how to cure himself and not needing anything was quite depressing, dangerous almost. Nowadays, emotions were entirely blended with needs. You either had them all or none. He tossed and turned and started to make bubbles with his saliva. 'Maybe I should eat some of those biscuits; they are not that bad ...' But he would never get up from the bed as that involved actually getting up from the bed.

'I will eat them tomorrow, first thing in the morning. I always forget why I didn't marry Piño; maybe I should give him a call tomorrow … first thing in the morning. Damn, I need to shit. Nah, tomorrow, first thing in the morning. What's the porker doing? Fuck, I need to sleep. Or maybe eat something. "Na nana nana … EverythingFrozen!" Mmmh, what shall I cook tomorrow? Shut up, Marxim! Did I lock downstairs? Yes, I did. Did I? He tried stopping the vortex of thoughts that always ended up bringing him to the darkest fantasies, but it was already too late. Senseless scenes of gruesome violence played in his head. Red and black punches and then funerals of people that never died. Then came the planning of situations in which he could use those deaths as an excuse to cry.

He imagined Chekhovich's funeral and how that would have made him feel. In his head, he talked to people he never met and didn't exist but people that he wanted to impress. He felt the parade of tears falling down his cheeks while giving a speech in the church. He mimed a little smile while talking with the guests about Chekhovich's adorable yet pathetic padded pants. Even in this head game, he complained about the exaggeration and limitation of present times while, with fondness, he remembered a time when society was kinder to men. A time when men could be proud of being men and didn't need padded pants because, 'after all, a small dick is still better than a pussy.' He shook his head and dried the rehearsed tears with his fist.

He felt guilty and dirty about having such thoughts, especially at his age when his brain should have been senile and serene. Before he could even notice, his hand was in his pants, and he was hard like he had never been in the last decade. Finally, he needed something again.

In the morning, all the dramas were forgotten, all the new farts, repressed. All were rested and energised. The kitchen was spotless. Lucretia was the last to arrive in the kitchen. She jumped on Marxim and popped a kiss on his cheek. She blushed when she saw the captain standing behind him.

'Morning gorgeous, do you want juice?' Marxim asked while whipping the pancake mix in one of those evergreen silver Ikea bowls.

'Ehm … nope,' she said, lowering her head and blushing even more.

Chekhovich saw the scene behind the book he again pretended to read, and it didn't take long to understand what happened – she slept with Marxim.

Although the pancakes were now fuming in front of him and the smells of vanilla and salmon filled the air, he couldn't think about anything else. Lucretia and Marxim were playing a sick father/husband/daughter game, and on top of that, in front of him!

'And on top of them, what do you want, Ceko?'

'Cinnamon cream cheese, *please*.' Chekhovich was a handsome man, and even with all his inferiority complexes, he knew he was hot stuff, at least hotter stuff than a 70-year-old catheter.

'I think it's better if we hurry up and get to Strontsky's headquarters as soon as possible,' Chekhovich said, moving the plate away from him. He still couldn't believe the old fuck snatched his girl and had the audacity to make him breakfast.

'Yeah, I agree. I think it's a great idea honestly,' Lucretia said, looking forward to getting out of the house.

'Oh, you do? Wow, we have so much in common,' Chekhovich answered.

Lucretia was both surprised and intrigued by his bitchy tone.

'Also, Marxim, I think Lucretia and I should go with the captain. Do you think that would be OK with you if I go with Lucretia … and you don't?'

'Sure, go together. Have a wank when she's not looking, whatever you guys prefer. I'd rather go with the captain, though,' Marxim said, blinking at piggy, 'just to keep an eye.'

Captain Grunter grunted in disappointment. He was no little piggy anymore. He even saw a semi-naked lady. He could take care of himself. Plus, he really wanted to go with Lucretia, whom he couldn't stop thinking about.

'Oh, you think you don't need me anymore?' Marxim asked while slapping and kissing the swine on his face. 'Alright then …'

'Yeah, Marxim, so you don't mind, yeah?' Chekhovich asked impatiently.

'Sure, I'll meet you there, guys,' Marxim said, looking at the captain with eyes filled with pride.

'You can take my car.' Chekhovich threw the keys at him, but they fell on the floor. He was livid, not only at Lucretia but also Marxim. The way Marxim looked at the pig almost had him in tears. Each time Marxim glanced at the captain, his eyes overflowed with love. Chekhovich's father never looked at him like that.

'Turd-engine,' Lucretia corrected Chekhovich.

'Yes, whatever, see you there, Marxim,' he said, giving a last bite to the pancake just to throw it back on the plate in disdain.

They all brushed their teeth, took their happy pills and left without even saying goodbye to Marxim, who was taking one final dump.

Lucretia was the last to come out. She almost fell on the trash, which she cursed and kicked aside.

'It was you, right? Trash people don't work on Fridays, genius. You never think things through.'

For a moment, Chekhovich pondered if he should have brought the bag along so he could throw it in the nearest dump point, but the captain grunted at them to jump up, and he immediately forgot about it. Out of sight, out of mind.

Lucretia sat first on the cold and prickly back of the pig. Chekhovich followed behind her, and off they went on another adventure. Calculating and scheming, Chekhovich thought that going without Marxim would give him a chance to spend more time with Lucretia, but the captain was flying so fast that he could barely catch a breath during the whole trip.

They ripped through the clouds and watched the landscape under them blend into a brownish mash. Grunter was nervous and awkward. Having Lucretia on top of him made him feel tingly, so he sped up, though he still needed to slow down and duck to avoid birds and insects, which would have smashed onto Lucretia's perfect face. He had to curb and go swiftly a couple of times, resulting in Lucretia rubbing on his back, back and forth, and Chekhovich poking against Lucretia's bum. When the captain finally landed, they were all very aroused and confused.

'Shall we wait for Marxim?' Lucretia asked, fixing her dress and cleaning the mosquito bits off her shoulder.

'Can't you think about anything else? Fucking Marxim, you and your daddy issues.'

'Hey, you are the one talking about fucking Marxim.'

'Yes, I think we should go without him unless you need him to take you by the hand.'

'It's OK, you have beautiful hands,' she said, looking straight into his eyes and interlocking her hand with his.

Chekhovich thought his heart was going to stop.

Immediately, Lucretia felt incredibly awkward as she realised that Captain Grunter was observing everything. No time to fix it; the damage was done. She dragged him away.

As the captain watched them walking all entwined and human, he also thought his heart would stop and that he was going to vomit – which would have been a bit bad for his image because he would have gobbled it up soon after. So, he waited and kept his distance from the two who walked towards the head office entrance, still hand in hand.

Chekhovich, pompous and erect like the Eiffel Tower, turned towards the captain. 'Maybe it's better if you wait here, so we don't raise suspicion. I will call you on the mind searcher if we are in trouble,' he said, winking.

Lucretia also turned and saw the sad superhero. Quickly from her purse, she fished one of the pancakes she stole from the house and threw it on the floor. The captain rushed to the snack. 'I think I'm in love,' he thought as he devoured the food.

When the two were close enough to the entrance, Lucretia turned into Lulu, her bitchier self. She dropped Chekhovich's hand and sashayed through the door.

The building had a high Gothic style and looked like a house of worship more than a head office. The front of the building had a distinctive glass façade that was reminiscent of the North Rose window of the Chartres Cathedral, only that instead of the Virgin Mary – Queen of Heaven, surrounded by prophets and kings – this one had portraits of workers and scenes of everyday life in the office: a guy that was late and was thrown out; a devilish girl wearing a sexy shirt and tempting a holy intern that got her lesson when she was abused in the bathroom, then a bathroom break that lasted more than five minutes being resolved in the destruction of all toilets, and finally, on top of everyone else, holy Strontsky with his arms wide open, holding a carrot and a stick.

'Hi, honey.' Lucretia entered the building and showed her A'lex's News pass to the guy at the reception. Chekhovich did the same and hurried up before he lost her in that unstoppable, shapeless flux of white shirts and suits. She stopped at the lift.

'Do you know where we are going?' he asked her, whispering.

'To the top. Morning babe, love your belt,' she said, smiling at a guy next to her. 'They are always at the top,' she mumbled, focussing on the doors opening.

And to the top, they went, asking for information from clueless interns until they finally found where Strontsky's office was. The bright colours that adorned and differentiated the floors and departments of the building abruptly ended in front of them. A black space – maybe a corridor, maybe the end of the world – was ahead of them. The last intern assured them the office was that way, so Chekhovich and Lucretia entered the void. Once they took the first step, no entrance or exit could be seen anymore. In this place with no end and no beginning, Lucretia again took Chekhovich's hand. She pulled him to the left and walked in that direction until she found a wall against which they both walked for what felt like the duration of an ad on YouTube – an eternity.

They didn't utter a word while walking. Chekhovich was pretty sure Lucretia was scared. He felt her hand tighten. In that midst of darkness, silence, and sweaty palms, he really felt her. He tightened his grip as well, pressing his phalanges on her knuckles and studying the anatomy of her right hand. He felt her little mole under his thumb and continued the journey to her wrist, where he found the rivers of her veins and nerves, which he massaged. They heard some clanking shoes fast approaching in that instant, and they stuck to the wall even more. They sucked in their bellies to better hide in that dark nothingness. As soon as the clanking was ahead of them, they followed it, trying to walk on their toes. When the clanking stopped, out of the darkness, a door opened, letting in an incredible amount of light. They noticed that the corridor was actually a huge room that expanded into the horizon and seemed to have no end. Still at the door, a guy took a tray with dirty dishes and left, closing the door and leaving the space in total darkness again.

Once the clanking-shoes-guy was only a weak echo, the two moved fast from far away before their brains could forget the distance to the door. They moved forward, being very cautious about leaving the wall. They had no perception of space. A couple of wrong steps, and they could have been wandering in the concrete oblivion for who knows how long. Chekhovich tripped over his own feet and fell on the floor, leaving his back defenceless to the void. Lucretia promptly lifted him and pushed him towards her before he got lost. They felt each other's bodies on their own. Chekhovich's enhanced pants perfectly fitted between Lucretia's legs that radiated with warmth. They breathed in and out and into each other's mouths. Lucretia took a deep breath so that Chekhovich could feel her ribs instead of her pot belly. They both waited for a kiss that never arrived in that timeless purgatory until Chekhovich went back to his place. Lucretia kept scouting with her hand for the door handle. It should not have been too far off from where they were now.

Without giving him a heads up, Lucretia took a big breath and opened the door, dragging her trusted helper along by the wrist.

'Make sure you write everything down, Chekhovich, everything. Good morning, Mr Strontsky. When I received your message, I was elated. I hope I didn't take too long. How can I help?' Lucretia said, confidently walking towards the desk.

Chekhovich looked right and left and had no idea how to look any less stupid and useless than he did right now.

'Write everything down, I told you! So hard to find good helpers today, right?'

Strontsky just gobbled down the last bite of his sandwich.

'Just hire interns ... they are free, at least,' Strontsky answered, showing some green between his teeth.

Strontsky's office was located just behind the thousand lights of the North Rose stained glass, which shone on him, colouring his face red and purple and creating a dramatic effect in the entire room, adorned like a baroque church. It had clusters of sculpted angels and twisted columns at each side of the room, embellished with an abundance of gilded Corinthian capitals. On the ceiling, a huge painting portraying the figure of a saint, whose face was composed of miniature paintings of other people. In the painting, the holy man bled golden coins out of cuts on his hands.

'Mornin' lady, what can I do you for?' Strontsky said, brushing the crumbs out of his grey handlebar moustache.

Strontsky was very tall and skinny. He had thick grey hair and piercing blue eyes – the kind of eyes you should never trust. His appearance was immaculate, Italian tailored black suit and padded red shoes. The hair, strong and bushy, was gelled to the back of his head. However, his beauty, just like the elegance of the room, was overpowered by the filth around him; crumpled up papers, scraps of food, plastic wrappings on the floor, and furniture adorned by half-eaten sandwiches and trays with cakes and pizza and various condiments. All this trash in front of their eyes clashed with the smell of the room, strawberry cotton candy.

'Hope I didn't interrupt your breakfast. I am Lucretia from A'lex's News,' she said, waiting for his reply. 'Yesterday, I received a message from one of your interns: 'Strontsky here, got big news, send hot girl,' she fake-read from her mind searcher.

Strontsky looked confused as he didn't remember calling his nephew's paper. However, he was old and not ready to admit his senility. He nodded, arrogant and serene. He was quite smitten by Lucretia. 'Why don't we get more comfortable,' he said, getting up and pointing at the talky-talky section. He sat first and watched every little movement Lucretia made on the way to the sofa. He enjoyed every little line stretching and retracting on her ribbed red dress and followed all the winces her mouth made. No rest, no safety, never – not even from the decrepit.

Chekhovich tried to join them, but Strontsky lifted his hand and blocked him without even looking at him. Instead, he snapped his fingers, immediately reaching the reception where hives of ambitious graduates waited eagerly for any order coming from the master. 'Drinks, now.'

'Yes, I called you because I heard you are doing a great job for my nephew. How about you come work for me here?'

'Ah! I can't. I signed a life contract with him. Plus …'

'I know why you want to stay. A'lex is young; he has big money, yes, but a small dick.'

'Yeah! Tell me about it!'

First drink

'Actually, now that I am here, as you know, A'lex's birthday is coming up, and we were thinking of surprising him with an

159

office make-over. Maybe give it a more historical outlook, you know? I loved the stained glass outside, great rhetoric; you on top of it with a stick and a carrot, just wow. Thank you, darling,' she said at the intern who delivered the alcohol.

'Carrot?' he asked, laughing so much he almost choked. 'What carrot? That's an orange stick!'

Lucretia hesitated until Chekhovich signalled her to start laughing.

'So, as I was saying, we want to make it less modern, maybe add paintings of all the greatest figures of the 21st century. Checking some files, I have found some great candidates to add to the collection. First, ahem … you, obviously.'

'Obviously. Then, who else?'

'Then on a second column under your picture, in much smaller print obviously, we would have Mr Ceteary, Miss Osumbor, Mr DüMal, Lady Boy–'

'How do you know that name?' Strontsky's tone swiftly changed.

Lucretia tried not to lose her cool but felt her heart racing, like when she drank ten espressos and had to fight for the last available cubicle in the office.

'A'lex mentioned her. Just the other day, we were talking about his childhood, his favourite TV shows, his favourite place on Earth – Thailand, of course, and I guess she just came up! He told me about how he enjoyed waiting for you after your meetings, how he loved spending quality time with you, getting lunch and buying cars and–'

'Diamond rings, that's right! I always underestimated how much those moments meant to him,' he said, proud of being such a loving father figure to A'lex.

Second drink

'Oh, how silly, I haven't mentioned it yet. I guess I always take for granted that everyone knows. A'lex is not only my boss in the office but at home as well! We are getting married,' she said, screaming and shaking her ring-less hand in front of him. 'So, you know the office makeover is a little gift for A'lex. I really want to impress him while I still have to,' she said, smiling at him.

'Of course, of course. Well, what do you need from me? More ideas, some money?' he said, snapping his finger. 'Money. Bring me money now.'

'You know what, how about some more drinks? We are gonna be family soon. Let's get to know each other.'

'Cancel money. I like you. What's your name? Bring drinks, now.' Strontsky snapped his fingers again.

Third drink

While Chekhovich sat, ignored and bored, Lucretia and the villain were getting acquainted, sipping martinis and daiquiris.

'So, why marry so young? You still have a lifetime of fucks to have.' Strontsky was eating her with his corrupted eyes.

'Are you trying to seduce me, Uncle? You know I am quite old-fashioned.'

'You are right. Let's do it only after the wedding!' Strontsky answered, and both of them clinked their glasses.

'What about you, ever gotten married? Any words of wisdom for a clueless little girl?'

'I almost got nailed once. Maybe A'lex was too young even to remember, but yes, there was a special lady in my life.'

'Interesting! Was that a lady or a Lady Boy–'

Strontsky interrupted her before she could finish and smiled, remembering his beautiful love. 'I think it might be good for you to know a bit of what's soon gonna be your family history so that you know what's coming your way.' He stopped smiling.

'I wouldn't want anything more,' answered Lucretia, sliding off her shoes and getting more comfortable.

'First of all, let's stop with the formalities. Just call me Daddy,' he said, getting closer and letting his rotten and cheesy breath linger in the air around Lucretia, who tried to keep the vomit down and focus on the faraway scent of strawberry candy floss.

'I was at one of those World Social Forums when I met her – the most beautiful woman I have ever seen. The topic of the meeting was globalisation and development … something like that. She was the brightest person in the room. By the way, just to make sure we are on the same page, what are your views about it?'

Chekhovich, alarmed by the highly intellectual question, felt the need to save Lucretia from her stupidity, but the superfluous man was superfluous once more.

'Well, it depends on which side of the world you are. To me, it's the best. How else would I get my £3 Ralph Lauren shirts? All is legit in love and economy. I am a very free girl; a free market kinda girl,' she said, enunciating each word with special emphasis. Hearing those words, Strontsky shivered.

'Exactly, but surprisingly, a free market doesn't really improve the economy.'

'No, you don't say!'

'Yes. If you don't put limitations on commerce and production, what you get is the opposite of efficiency.'

'But then again, if you put too many limitations, then you give a chance to get rich to any little developing country. Is that what you want, Daddy?' Lucretia pouted like a child who's just been denied her dessert. Although Strontsky didn't know what love was, he was pretty sure it was something like what his dick was feeling for Lucretia right now.

'Of course not, my little girl, but the point is, how can we create new economies without experimenting? We must be like … chemists, like chefs. How do you think pizza was made? A guy had too much pineapple, and now it's history.'

Fourth and fifth drinks

'Everybody only had those tired ideas of the past: inflation, maybe start a conflict, switch the production areas, blah blah. But she had all the answers. I swear to Manson, she had everything. Brains, looks, boobs, dick, everything.' He took a meaningful break to remember the past and hiccup. 'Unfortunately, we found out she was in cahoots. Cahoots is a funny word, isn't it? So, we had to cancel her. She was really fond of A'lex. Even if he has always been a weakling.' He stopped to blow raspberries. 'But you love my boy, don't you?'

'Apple of my eye,' she replied, fluttering her eyelashes like a butterfly flapping its wings.

'You know he used to be fat? He should be very grateful to have such a good piece of pussy like you. Well, anybody should.'

She looked at Chekhovich. 'Hope you are still taking notes.'

'Yeah, bitch! Take notes,' Strontsky shouted at Chekhovich, laughing and chugging the rest of his drink. 'He was such a fat little guy, always sucking on some ribs and steaks. I used to tell him all the time, you keep eating those, you are gonna turn into a pig.'

Sixth drink

Lucretia laughed so much she spat her drink. She was actually having a good time. That was the problem with alcohol, it made you have fun with anyone.

Chekhovich, who was utterly bored and sober, cleared his voice a couple of times before Lucretia heard him.

'Daddy, where's the bathroom?'

He snapped his finger, and immediately, an intern came to escort her.

When Lucretia arrived at the bathroom, she was dazed. In front of her was a squat toilet, which was basically just a hole in the ground without any door or divider to shield the last shred of dignity of Strontsky's employees. She tried to pee without wetting herself, cursing her haemorrhoids, badly inflamed by the amount of alcohol she consumed. As she let the wind pass, a squirt of blood dripped down the white tiles of the wall. Toilet paper was handed parsimoniously, only four squares per drop. Lucretia prioritised her genitals and left the bloodbath as it was. Ashamed, she washed her hands. While she was leaving, a group of office girls entered gossiping about the new supervisor and who's ass he had to eat to get the position. One of them screamed as she saw the blood. 'Gals, it's a message. No more bathroom breaks today!

'Fab, let's go then.'

'Yas gurl! Let's go back to our desks, and let's be fucking productive!'

In the meantime, Chekhovich was listening to the essential truth of life – the one that nobody wants you to know. Strontsky was telling him about how any lack of beauty and power could be overcome by great ambition and a big dick. Everyone could turn gay in front of a big dick, and everyone was gay with someone else's bum.

'So, you take them from behind and then like-' Strontsky cleared his throat and changed his tone when Lucretia came back. 'Finally, my beautiful. So, what did you think of it?' He turned to Chekhovich one last time and mimed a blowjob while he accompanied Lucretia back on the couch.

'Ehm, loved the design, so futuristic, very communal. Scandinavian?'

'I knew you'd love it. You don't look like a girl who's afraid to squat.'

'No pain, no drain, right? Yeah, so … great.'

'I love this little girl!' Strontsky said to Chekhovich.

He snapped his fingers again, and more drinks appeared.

Seventh drink

'Let me tell you about a bit of my architectural philosophy. It might help you with your little office makeover project. Take a bathroom, for example. You think it's just a crapper, but what I ask you is: tell me how you poop, and I will tell you who you are.'

Chekhovich closed his eyes just for a moment and thought it was only in his head that this conversation was taking place.

'See, the relation between materiality and function helps interpret social identity. If you know how things make people, then you can change people through objects. Make sense, no? For example, "German toilets are the key to the horrors of the Third Reich. People who can build things like that are capable of anything." Do you know who said that?'

'Erica Jong!' Chekhovich immediately woke up, eager to finally join the conversation. Of course, he googled the answer. With the last generation mind searcher pretending to be smart was never easier.

'Yes, yes, good boy, take a cookie and fuck off.' He went back to talking to Lucretia. 'Now think about the three types of toilet designs we have in the West: the traditional German toilet, which presents an examination plate almost for a "lay-and-display" while the hole in which the faeces disappear after flushing, is way up front, then we have la toilette Française, the French shitter, which instead has a hole far in the back so that the discharge may disappear as soon as possible, like "au revoir monsieur la merde." Then, at last, we have the American toilet, which can be seen as a mediation between the two different aforementioned thrones. The toilet is full of water so that the turds are still visible to be watched but left free to roam anywhere they want, just like Americans. Now, just think about the symbolic way in which these three countries are getting rid of the shit. A certain ideological and cultural perception is clearly detectable, don't you think? If you may, this trinity can be interpreted as Germany with its NEIN, NEIN, NEIN thoroughness; France with the revolutionary radicalism – *Ceci n'est pas une merde*; and then America with its liberalism.'

'OK … so what's with squatting?'

'I have been raised respecting the fact that what comes with great sacrifice always brings a bigger reward … for me, most of the time. I am just so impressed by those countries with dictatorships so strict they don't even let people sit to take a shit. I find it very inspiring. Less shitting, more working,' he said, lusting after Lucretia's feet rubbing against each other.

The more Strontsky talked about toilets and shit, the more Lucretia felt the atrocious smell of his breath. Lucretia snapped her fingers. 'Oh, come now, Daddy, stop talking about toilets. All a girl wants to talk about is love. Please, keep talking about Lady B. What happened with her?' She was alternating her normal voice to a very squeaky virgin-slut tone. Strontsky loved it and snapped his fingers.

Eighth drink

Crossing his legs, he reminisced about the dark part of his love story, which was as tart as the acid reflux he tried to keep down between each sip. 'You know the usual, the worst tragedy, the sweetest love story. Like Romeo and Juliet, I believed in a free market; she believed in freedom from work. She was so against the performance principle.'

Lucretia didn't know what he was talking about, so she did what she knew would work, kept nodding, and waited for things to figure themselves out.

'What's so wrong about an honest 12-hour working day for minimum wage? We made people happy; they loved working. The more they worked, the more they spent, and it made those few couple of hours of free time after work so much sweeter. In those hours, they could be whoever they wanted, affectionate parents, passionate lovers, or inspired artists. Obviously, most of them just turned out to be violent drunks and comatose spectators, either of their own lives or television. So now tell me, what would violent drunks do if they only worked four hours per day instead of 12? They would wreck the entire world, that's what they'd do. We kept murderers too tired to go out and kill people, and we kept wives from cheating on their husbands. Well, unless they cheated at work. In that case, we actually-

'Yup, totally. How about a double date? She sounds lovely! She still in London?' Lucretia said, hiccupping.

'Well, she's here and there, you know,' Strontsky said, smiling and stretching his hand to a nearby salmontella cheese sandwich. 'Here and there,' he kept repeating to himself between each bite.

'Yeah, but where?'

'I said here,' he pointed at one of the columns in the room, 'and there,' he said, laughing and pointing at the other.

Lucretia, tipsy and bewildered, punched Strontsky's arm, making his sandwich spill on his beard. 'Daddy! What did you do that for?' She laughed, but she was actually terrified.

'What should have I done?' Strontsky was amused by Lucretia's reaction, not many girls would react the way she did. 'She was gonna spill all our secrets to the others, and I told her, the bears of silence treat the fruit of ...' He laughed alone. 'No, I told her the fruit of peach brings the fuck!' He waited a bit to reorder his thoughts. 'The tree of silence bears the fruit of peace.' He swallowed another bite.

Lucretia clapped her hands, acknowledging his hard work. 'Who ... who was she gonna tell those secrets to?'

Ninth drink

The intern came in shaking cocktails and pouring them in the crystal glasses. Strontsky told the guy that he was not to disturb until *further coitus*.

'Look, Lulu, can I call you Lulu?' he said, cleaning his mouth and carelessly throwing the leftovers of his sandwich on the floor. 'I know why you are asking all these questions, stop pretending.' He got closer to Lucretia with feline agility. 'You want me. You just have to ask for it. Women always do, anyway.'

Strontsky's face was dangerously close to Lucretia, who was now able to inspect his nauseating cavities.

'Stronzo,' Lucretia whispered before giving him a blow straight to the nose, 'that's not what I asked.' She laughed, proud of herself.

Chekhovich, who had fallen asleep around drink five or six, was startled awake when he heard Strontsky's screams.

'Fucking slut! What's your problem?' Strontsky said, looking for a handkerchief for his bleeding nose.

'What have you done, Lucretia? We must call the captain, now!' Chekhovich frantically mumbled.

'I really hoped the alcohol would erase the stench of his breath, but it actually enhanced it,' Lucretia said, checking her head wasn't dirty with blood and greasy salmontella crumbs.

Strontsky spat the blood on the floor, already sullied by his beastly manners and greed. He tried snapping his fingers to call reception. Unfortunately, the blood made his fingers slide against each other, and he couldn't produce the sound. He slowly walked towards the door. He had to do everything by himself in this damn building.

'Did you really have to do that? Why didn't you call me?' said Chekhovich, walking nervously around Lucretia.

'You were just there; there was no time. That stench was killing me. It was either vomit in his mouth or hit him, and I am a lady.' Lucretia noticed Strontsky walking away and tried to grab him.

'I am gonna fucking kill you, motherfucking bitch,' Strontsky said, pulling away from Lucretia. He tried snapping his fingers once again, but it was still not working.

'Where are you going, Daddy? Let's have another drink,' Lucretia said, holding him by the collar.

'You are gonna end up in those columns too. I will tell A'lex.'

'Nah, I will just eat him up and make everything nice.'

'You stupid bitch, you think sucking him off will hold him back. He's family.'

'No, I meant eat him up like … like a pig.' She couldn't hold the laughter any longer. 'He's a pig. Your nephew, A'lex, is a pig!'

Chekhovich came from behind and struck a blow at Strontsky's head, leaving him senseless on the littered floor. He was not sure this move would have worked, but he saw it so many times in movies, it must have been true.

'That was fucking weird. What did you do that for?' asked Lucretia.

'It was either you or him. Hun.'

'Uh, so you do love me a bit?' Lucretia said, getting closer to Chekhovich with her legs wide open and Strontsky in between them. 'You love me, Ceko?' she asked, lifting her dress, moving her panties aside, and pissing on Strontsky.

'What's wrong with you?'

'Like he said, I am not afraid to squat!'

'He will probably enjoy that. Why are you so weird?' Chekhovich said, disgusted and confused. He didn't understand Lucretia's madness, not the least bit.

Lucretia backed away from him and went back on the red velvety sofa, drunk and offended, wondering why what she considered hilarious and original was weird and unacceptable for anyone else. All the looks she ever received were either looks of pity or lust or looks from people she didn't care about, so it didn't really matter. Laying her head on the cushion where she had earlier spilt a bit of drink, she thought of the night before when she spent interminable moments contemplating the universe in the captain's eyes who – salivating on the pillow – looked at her like she always wanted to be looked at; just as if she were there.

Chekhovich took off his belt and tried to tie Strontsky's hands together. He tried to avoid touching Lucretia's piss, but unfortunately, the evil guy's suit was drenched. He thought of how that weirdness disgusted and aroused him at the same time. She made his blood boil. What was there to do to forget about her? Maybe he could have called one of the Hans from the other night. Maybe killing Marxim would have had her so upset she would have run into his arms, kissed him like he was the only guy at a girls-only sleepover. He had to forget her, he kept telling himself as he tied the belt tighter, and Stronstky's hands began to look purple. Maybe only euthanasia would have helped him.

'By the way, where's Marxim?' Lucretia asked, and Chekhovich spat fury out of his eyes.

***

After Marxim finished cleaning the kitchen, he gave all the leftovers to A'lex, who was now responding only to a strong whistle instead of his human name. Then, he hoovered all the food from the floor, the same floor that only days before was smeared with …

'Shit! Stop it, you silly sausage!' Marxim shouted as A'lex tried to pull his pants down; soon, he bit his tongue and pleaded forgiveness from A'lex. How could he be so insensible? A'lex oinked and grunted and didn't even care about what Marxim said. He had become such a friendly and playful pig. Marxim was proud of him, proud of the whole little fighting crime family that fate had brought together. He thought about this for the entire length of the long hot shower he took. What was everyone doing for the Feaster Break? Should they spend it together? He set an alarm on his mind recorder: 'Organise FB with the gang. Buy more lizard eggs.'

He got dressed and looked in the mirror. For once, he didn't judge his wrinkled yellow face and the weird contrast it made with his ginger hair. Instead, he admired his eyes, his emerald-green eyes that always set him apart from all those average browns and cruel blues.

He analysed his belly, inflating and deflating it a couple of times, and ended up playing with the lard that hung outside his pants. He watched the time, 11 a.m. *Life was too short to be in a hurry*, he thought. He walked downstairs slowly, peacefully ignoring all that was around him, all the gifts that the younger captain made him for Father's Days, Valentine's Days, and birthdays. He made a little snack for the captain, carefully covering the sandwich with a thick layer of film wrap.

Marxim grabbed the keys from the plastic countertop of the kitchen. As he got out, he bumped into the trash bag on the porch. He walked towards the crap mobile … or was it the turd engine? He couldn't remember the exact words Lucretia used to describe the car, but they felt so very right each time he entered that old X5. As he drove on the bumpy road, his mind roamed the past, to when he visited his grandparents in Inverness, for the last time. It was his birthday, the 8th of March 1991, and it was snowing. On the ride, what was all very bucolic soon became a Christmas picture postcard. An abnormal snowstorm blocked the city. People wrapped up in their warmest clothes talked about how the world was doomed. Shrugging their shoulders, the old ones repeated that there were no more middle seasons, that the cattle would have frozen, and that the cheese used to taste different. The wind was icy. Reckless children ran outside despite their mothers' orders to go back into the house. Some of them even dared to touch the snow before their worried mothers rushed outside and dragged them in, swearing all of Manson's Kingdom down. The trees, the grass, and the stones were covered in snow. You could almost feel the suffering of those timid green buds crushed under the white violence.

Driving to his beloved son, Marxim turned on the music. 'Fucking Mozart again. Can't we just have something else for once? Nope. Piano Concerto No. 9, KV 271, II: Andantino. In what kind of world do people know every Mozart composition by heart but nothing about anything else?'

***

'You remind me of my daughter, you know?' Strontsky said, looking at Lucretia's boobs.

'Oh yeah? Did you try to have sex with her as well?'

'Oh … no? No!'

'She's into techno jazz and crack cocaine?'

Strontsky kept shaking his head without realising he was still staring at the breasts. 'No, she's a strong, independent woman who needs no …'

'Let me guess, no crack cocaine? Of course! Everyone is always better than me, right?' Lucretia said, looking at Chekhovich.

'What's this obsession with crack cocaine?' Chekhovich asked.

'I mean, it's only amazing. Like a shot of coffee and a knock in the ass at the same time.' Lucretia's eyes sparkled.

As the final begging was derailing from its initial intent, Strontsky cleared his voice and started over. 'As I was saying, you remind me of my daughter. You get it?' Once he made sure he had everyone's attention, he went back to a more pious and humble tone. 'She's kind, and she's so passionate … her favourite colour is pink – only nice people like pink! I am sure you like pink too, right, Lucretia? Please be reasonable. I have a family; I have employees. What would happen to them? My daughter would agree. She would not kill me, she would … kill him, instead. I mean, look at his stupid man-bun. He's kinda asking for it, don't you think so?'

'Again? Don't try and blame the victim here. This guy is a proud metrosexual. He's probably bad in bed; he deserves the man bun. He needs the man bun. He might pass as a normal person without it, someone whose self-confidence comes from a big dick or his intellect, not from his internet-bought spiritualism. If he stopped wearing a man bun, he would be lying not only to himself but to the rest of the world. Just imagine the disappointment of finding him on alonenomore. com and thinking damn! Only to go out with him and find out ... damn ...' she said, rolling her eyes.

'OK, look, the point is, I don't wanna die. I am still in my prime. I haven't even begun—'

'Meh ... not interested, Daddy.'

'My daughter needs me. She won't survive my death. She's very fragile.'

'What's her name?'

Strontsky was uncertain for a moment. 'Hola,' he continued, 'her name is Hola.'

'Hola. Really? Like hola chica estas muy rica? Lol, try harder next time. Captain, do the honours.'

Chekhovich pulled her arm and whispered in her ear.

'Oh right. That was awkward.'

'You must believe me. I am not lying to you. You kill me now; you doom my daughter, Lady Boyce's daughter! You wanted to know about her, you fucking bitch. If you kill me, you get nothing.'

The captain came in, roaring like the hurricanes of the apocalypse. The man he saw in A'lex's memory was slightly different from the pathetic mess he had in front of him. However, the mean blue eyes were the same. Strontsky's moustache was now white and candid. Still, he had not been granted the redeeming qualities that old age awarded.

Strontsky's existence disgusted him deeply. His creeping fear offended him.

'Stop, please, I'll tell you everything! How I dissected her body after she threatened to broadcast the timeline to … no! Don't do that! What are you doing?

Something felt off, but neither Lucretia nor Chekhovich dared to say a word. Where was Marxim? As the captain walked the walk towards him, he began to look more human than ever. His eyes turned nuclear green, and the world was forever changed.

'Please, let Daddy go.' In the room, they could hear Strontsky's cheekbones almost crumble.

'Blessed be you, Lucretia in tears! Blessed be you, Lucretia, in fear! Blessed be your death! Blessed be Manson! Blessed be Manson!'

Those were the Strontsky's last words, whose face deformed from his pathetic cries — soon turned skinless and bloodied, and with acute laments, tears of blood dripped on the carpet from his now empty sockets. In Strontsky's agony, the captain lived through the pain that his kind had endured since the beginning of times. He became the chopped limbs seasoned with salt and lemon, the bellies fried and sizzling for the little one's breakfast, and the old ones' vices and whims. In his head played the noise the hoofs made while walking the walk of death, clicking on the cold and jarring metal as they entered the slaughterhouse. The bangs of the remorseless gunshots to the brain, the electrodes, the bolt pistols, the slashed throats. He smelled the terror and the gas used to render the pigs unconscious. He smelled the coppery scent flowing from the carotids sliced open for exsanguination. He felt the warmth of the pig scalding and the burnt smell coming from the torch used to remove hair.

While Strontsky's leather clothes swelled and ripped, his back curved, and his bones broke, the captain kept seeing millions of pigs decapitated and eviscerated. No remorse, no pain. He saw his brothers and sisters cut in halves and hoisted on a rail while their organs were ripped and thrown away. He thought of humans, deboning all the fathers and every mother that had ever lived. He tried clearing his head, but those atrocities clung to him. All the excruciating suffering his kind had endured made him feel like one of them.

Marxim came into his thoughts. He saved him, became a father to him. He remembered the warmth of his hugs and the sweetness of the apple rot he always gave him for breakfast. Yes, Marxim became a father to him, but only after he sold all his family and probably ate some of them too. Where was Marxim now? He was again alone in the world – enraged about the hypocrisy of love, a love that doesn't protect but devours, a desire that pines and bites to the bone, that chews till you are an indistinguishable matter in a pit of acid. He wanted to destroy Strontsky and all of his cohorts, annihilate everybody that had ever savoured any kind of meat.

But Lucretia was looking at him, beautiful, smart, and kind Lucretia. Had her mouth ever been a graveyard of innocent souls? Had her full and red lips been death for his kind? Next to her, Chekhovich, the intellectual. Did he deserve to be punished? He was just weak, a slave of his desires and the system that imposed flesh as a symbol of life. How could he have known better if nobody around him was better? He didn't deserve to be pitied, but he didn't deserve death either.

When Strontsky's cries seemed to have ended, a last louder-than-hate scream came out at the unison with hundreds of other shouts coming from the building. Strontsky's vital yet meaningless little helpers that so greatly accepted the scorn and the injustices for the hope that one day eventually, maybe they could have followed his success, joined him in his fate.

Lucretia and Chekhovich were unaware of what was happening. Where was Marxim?

The two backed away towards the door, trying not to stumble on any shreds of skins, bones, and clothes. They were not scared yet, just curious about the screams they heard.

'Wait, let me see if everything is OK,' said Chekhovich, who cautiously looked outside. Nothing unusual in the black nothingness of the corridor. He looked right and left a couple of times before a shrieking sound reverberated in the air. Running like fury, a big four-legged animal came in his direction. The beast, a pinkish swine with black spots on the back, stopped in front of Strontsky's office. He looked up and down for a few seconds and smelled the carpet. It was as if he had forgotten what he came to do. He gave a distracted look at Chekhovich and screamed in his face before continuing running and shrieking.

'Lucretia,' Chekhovich said, pulling her arm, still shocked. Lucretia didn't move and didn't talk. She was staring at the dollop of inhuman remains, which was still moving. Lucretia gagged and pulled Chekhovich so close that his dick was basically in her underwear.

They stared at the abomination in front of them. They experienced the abjection, the repulsion and revulsion, watching all those organs and blood and the stench on the floor and inside the bodies, they prided themselves in keeping like temples.

The captain's eyes were still acid green and pointed at the shapeless mass, which kept moving like dancing mayonnaise on a plate. Finally, out of the mess, a little pig came out, adorable and cute, until it started eating the skin and organs his previous human body expelled.

'What the fuck is going on. Another one?' Lucretia said, with the desperation of a single about to have a triplet.

'There's more … in the corridor; I saw another.'

'Captain, what's happening?' Lucretia asked, running to him. On her knees, she caressed Grunter's face in a mixture of love and terror. 'Wake up, Captain … what have you done?'

Chekhovich pulled Lucretia away, and together, they walked to the North Rose. Lucretia opened the window. Outside in the huge courtyard, tables and MacBooks stayed untouched while thousands of wild pigs ran in circles into each other, took dumps, and had asthma and panic attacks.

The belts broke loose, clothes ripped, and tails came out of the prisoner's backs. Hands transformed into hoofs. The bums so carefully waxed and shaved with Swiss precision for years turned into hairy hams and the abs so painfully gained turned into bacon. One pig assaulted the snack machine. Some tried in vain to use the laptops with their hoofs. Others seized the moment and went on to rape the co-workers that always teased them at the Christmas parties and those that constantly critiqued their reports. Lucretia and Chekhovich kept staring, mesmerised and speechless. Gradually, the shrieks were replaced by grunts, and some of the pigs even took naps.

Had the perpetrators become the victims?

Lucretia and Chekhovich remained silent. They went there to get answers, and yes, everybody took for granted that an execution could have taken place, maybe even two, if things got rockier. What happened instead was completely unexpected, an evolution of the species.

Hours after, Lucretia and Chekhovich were still in awe, looking out the window at the animal world documentary playing before their own eyes. They still did not know what to think and what to do. Captain Grunter was their ride, and he was still catatonic.

Where was Marxim?

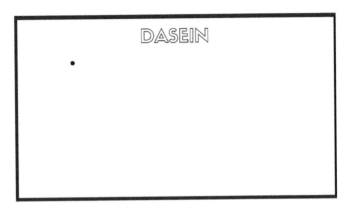

DASEIN

Marxim had never really thought about death, and although bits and pieces had begun leaving his body, he always saw that as more of an evolution than the last checkpoint. He had quite a romantic view of things and what was always meant to be. Like, some people falling in love with their soulmates or like people dying young. Some things are inevitable. He never got married because he believed in death more than love.

Also, he was never that rich and bored to organise a wedding party with the hundreds of fascist relatives he usually hid from or pretended not to see at family gatherings and blocked on social media. He was fine with spending his life alone. Things changed when little Grunter came around. He understood he was not destined for romantic love but something bigger, so yes, he sucked that occasional dick, but he never looked for anything more. He didn't need it. He spent that morning celebrating his decrepit looks, accepting the fact that there was no point in battling a fight he could not win. He could not shield himself from his tired hanging skin and his callous hands. However, when another car, a yellow FIAT 500, came full speed towards him and made him crash against an old oak, that was a surprise for Marxim, and he felt a bit betrayed.

During the impact with the tree, acorns fell on the mangled metal of the hood. Shreds of windshield shone like diamonds on Marxim's head. His face was glued to the horn. Copious amounts of blood fell down the steering wheel and onto his legs which he could not move. No sound came out of his moving lips, and even if it did, he could not have heard it because of the continuous and deafening honking noise. He felt trapped in his own body, yet he did not feel any pain. Another acorn fell on his head and rolled to the side, ending up on the passenger seat. Marxim smiled.

He had not really thought about death before that day, and he never thought his would be so depressing and lonely. He wanted to die of a heart attack after eating too many fried pizzas or with a heart stroke during the night. He wanted death to really desire him, like the seductive call of a new lover inviting you to share the bed with him or like the asphyxiating hugs of his mother. Marxim was robbed from his romantic idea of death, but at the same time, dying, he had finally reached the existential authenticity of being alive. As if all those routines of waking up, going to work, working, eating but not too much, sleeping, and repeating had precluded him from engaging with the personal experience of what it means to be alive. The forgetfulness of being and the manipulated truths and desires had estranged him from the dimension where the essence of being remained veiled. However, when confronted with his own mortality, he finally transcended, reaching the state of being rather than existing.

***

In the coldest hours of the night, a dog, a beautiful black Labrador, walked around Marxim's farm. All the lights were off, and apart from the shrieking noise unfamiliar to the dog, nobody seemed to be awake. Hungry and curious, or maybe just in the mood for shopping, the dog stole a garbage bag leaning against a red door. He dragged the bag for a few miles just in case the shrieking sound wanted to steal his spoils.

Rubbing on the unpaved rocky way, the bag tore apart and left multiple pieces of trash on the way: a pink bottle of conditioner for STRONG MEN with fragile hair, a sock with a hole, an old Tupperware with a blue lid, a green toothbrush, shreds of receipts, the greasy plastic wrap of smoked salmon which the dog licked ferociously. For less than a mile, the trail of plastic was everything left of Marxim, an extension of himself. Even after his death, these objects represented the remains of his time on Earth, potentially forever. He was not only in the hearts of those who loved him, but he was in the farm which he built with only his powerful hands. He was in his bed that still smelled like him, and he was in the amount of waste he was now responsible for. Considering how long his cream, shampoos, conditioner bottles, as well his hair/tooth/ toilet brushes would have been around, either in stinky landfills or immense oceans, his time on Earth was going to be eternal.

Marxim, like many other dead, had it easy. He was going to receive a beautiful burial and coloured chrysanthemums at least a couple of times every year for a couple of years before everyone forgot him or died. What about those objects he cherished so much and worked hard to get? What about those little plastic orphans doomed to be floating around in sewers and fish stomachs forever? Did those objects that served Marxim so diligently deserve to spend eternity in a landfill?

The night was leaving the sky, and the dog stopped, for he was tired. He dug into the remaining trash inside the abused bag. He licked his whiskers and insistently poked around a package with a red ribbon. He wrestled the package until the ribbon gave up and the paper was wet and full of holes. A gentle breeze lifted the ribbon that flew over the dog, along with pieces of Styrofoam and dust. The dog, uninterested in the suggestive scenography, devoured the raisin and rosemary cookies. The wind carried the ribbon high into the sky. It was invisible now. Nobody was there to honour its departure; no one wondered what it might have seen. But it was gone. Amen.